Arthur Conan Doyle

Danger!

DOGMA

Arthur Conan Doyle

Danger!

ISBN/EAN: 9783955075217

Auflage: 1

Erscheinungsjahr: 2013

Erscheinungsort: Bremen, Deutschland

Arthur Conan Doyle

Danger!

DOGMA

Arthur Conan Doyle

Danger!

CLASSIC PAGES

PREFACE

The Title story of this volume was written about eighteen months before the outbreak of the war, and was intended to direct public attention to the great danger which threatened this country. It is a matter of history how fully this warning has been justified and how, even down to the smallest details, the prediction has been fulfilled. The writer must, however, most thankfully admit that what he did not foresee was the energy and ingenuity with which the navy has found means to meet the new conditions. The great silent battle which has been fought beneath the waves has ended in the repulse of an armada far more dangerous than that of Spain.

It may be objected that the writer, feeling the danger so strongly, should have taken other means than fiction to put his views before the authorities. The answer to this criticism is that he did indeed adopt every possible method, that he personally approached leading naval men and powerful editors, that he sent three separate minutes upon the danger to various public bodies, notably to the Committee for National Defence, and that he touched upon the matter in an article in *The Fortnightly Review*. In some unfortunate way subjects of national welfare are in this country continually subordinated to party politics, so that a self-evident proposition, such as the danger of a nation being fed from without, is waved aside and ignored, because it will not fit in with some general political shibboleth. It is against this tendency that we have to guard in the future, and we have to bear in mind that the danger may recur, and that the remedies in the text (the only remedies ever proposed) have still to be adopted. They are the sufficient encouragement of agriculture, the making of adequate Channel tunnels, and the provision of submarine merchantmen, which, on the estimate of Mr. Lake, the American designer, could be made up to 7,000 ton burden at an increased cost of about 25 per cent. It is true that in this war the Channel tunnels would not have helped us much in the matter of food, but were France a neutral and supplies at liberty to come via Marseilles from the East, the difference would have been enormous.

Apart from food however, when one considers the transports we have needed, their convoys, the double handling of cargo, the interruptions of traffic from submarines or bad weather, the danger and suffering of the wounded, and all else that we owe to the insane opposition to the Channel tunnels, one questions whether there has ever been an example of national stupidity being so rapidly and heavily punished. It is as clear as daylight even now, that it will take years to recover all our men and material from France, and that if the tunnel (one will suffice for the time), were at once set in hand, it might be ready to help in this task and so free shipping for the return of the Americans. One thing however, is clear. It is far too big and responsible and lucrative an undertaking for a private company, and it should be carried out and controlled by Government, the proceeds being used towards the war debt.

Arthur Conan Doyle.

August 24th, Crowborough.

I. DANGER! [1]
BEING THE LOG OF CAPTAIN JOHN SIRIUS

It is an amazing thing that the English, who have the reputation of being a practical nation, never saw the danger to which they were exposed. For many years they had been spending nearly a hundred millions a year upon their army and their fleet. Squadrons of Dreadnoughts costing two millions each had been launched. They had spent enormous sums upon cruisers, and both their torpedo and their submarine squadrons were exceptionally strong. They were also by no means weak in their aerial power, especially in the matter of seaplanes. Besides all this, their army was very efficient, in spite of its limited numbers, and it was the most expensive in Europe. Yet when the day of trial came, all this imposing force was of no use whatever, and might as well have not existed. Their ruin could not have been more complete or more rapid if they had not possessed an ironclad or a regiment. And all this was accomplished by me, Captain John Sirius, belonging to the navy of one of the smallest Powers in Europe, and having under my command a flotilla of eight vessels, the collective cost of which was eighteen hundred thousand pounds. No one has a better right to tell the story than I.

I will not trouble you about the dispute concerning the Colonial frontier, embittered, as it was, by the subsequent death of the two missionaries. A naval officer has nothing to do with politics. I only came upon the scene after the ultimatum had been actually received. Admiral Horli had been summoned to the Presence, and he asked that I should be allowed to accompany him, because he happened to know that I had some clear ideas as to the weak points of England, and also some schemes as to how to take advantage of them. There were only four of us present at this meeting — the King, the Foreign Secretary, Admiral Horli, and myself. The time allowed by the ultimatum expired in forty-eight hours.

I am not breaking any confidence when I say that both the King and the Minister were in favour of a surrender. They saw no possibility of standing up against the colossal power of Great Britain. The Minister had drawn up an acceptance of the British terms, and the King sat with it before him on the table. I saw the tears of anger and humiliation run down his cheeks as he looked at it.

"I fear that there is no possible alternative, Sire," said the Minister. "Our envoy in London has just sent this report, which shows that the public and the Press are more united than he has ever known them. The feeling is intense, especially since the rash act of Malort in desecrating the flag. We must give way."

The King looked sadly at Admiral Horli.

"What is your effective fleet, Admiral?" he asked.

"Two battleships, four cruisers, twenty torpedoboats, and eight submarines," said the Admiral.

The King shook his head.

"It would be madness to resist," said he.

"And yet, Sire," said the Admiral, "before you come to a decision I should wish you to hear Captain Sirius, who has a very definite plan of campaign against the English."

"Absurd!" said the King, impatiently. "What is the use? Do you imagine that you could defeat their vast armada?"

"Sire," I answered, "I will stake my life that if you will follow my advice you will, within a month or six weeks at the utmost, bring proud England to her knees."

There was an assurance in my voice which arrested the attention of the King.

"You seem self-confident, Captain Sirius."

"I have no doubt at all, Sire."

"What then would you advise?"

"I would advise, Sire, that the whole fleet be gathered under the forts of Blankenberg and be protected from attack by booms and piles. There they can stay till the war is over. The eight submarines, however, you will leave in my charge to use as I think fit."

"Ah, you would attack the English battleships with submarines?"

"Sire, I would never go near an English battleship."

"And why not?"

"Because they might injure me, Sire."

"What, a sailor and afraid?"

"My life belongs to the country, Sire. It is nothing. But these eight ships — everything depends upon them. I could not risk them. Nothing would induce me to fight."

"Then what will you do?"

"I will tell you, Sire." And I did so. For half an hour I spoke. I was clear and strong and definite, for many an hour on a lonely watch I had spent in thinking out every detail. I held them enthralled. The King never took his eyes from my face. The Minister sat as if turned to stone.

"Are you sure of all this?"

"Perfectly, Sire."

The King rose from the table.

"Send no answer to the ultimatum," said he. "Announce in both houses that we stand firm in the face of menace. Admiral Horli, you will in all respects carry out that which Captain Sirius may demand in furtherance of his plan. Captain Sirius, the field is clear. Go forth and do as you have said. A grateful King will know how to reward you."

I need not trouble you by telling you the measures which were taken at Blankenberg, since, as you are aware, the fortress and the entire fleet were destroyed by the British within a week of the declaration of war. I will confine myself to my own plans, which had so glorious and final a result.

The fame of my eight submarines, *Alpha*, *Beta*,

Gamma, *Theta*, *Delta*, *Epsilon*, *Iota*, and *Kappa*, have spread through the world to such an extent that people have begun to think that there was something peculiar in their form and capabilities. This is not so. Four of them, the *Delta*, *Epsilon*, *Iota*, and *Kappa*, were, it is true, of the very latest model, but had their equals (though not their superiors) in the navies of all the great Powers. As to *Alpha*, *Beta*, *Gamma*, and *Theta*, they were by no means modern vessels, and found their prototypes in the old F class of British boats, having a submerged displacement of eight hundred tons, with heavy oil engines of sixteen hundred horse-power, giving them a speed of eighteen knots on the surface and of twelve knots submerged. Their length was one hundred and eighty-six and their breadth twenty-four feet. They had a radius of action of four thousand miles and a submerged endurance of nine hours. These were considered the latest word in 1915, but the four new boats exceeded them in all respects. Without troubling you with precise figures, I may say that they represented roughly a twenty-five per cent. advance up on the older boats, and were fitted with several auxiliary engines which were wanting in the others. At my suggestion, instead of carrying eight of the very large Bakdorf torpedoes, which are nineteen feet long, weigh half a ton, and are charged with two hundred pounds of wet gun-cotton, we had tubes designed for eighteen of less than half the size. It was my design to make myself independent of my base.

And yet it was clear that I must have a base, so I made arrangements at once with that object. Blankenberg was the last place I would have chosen.

Why should I have a *port* of any kind? Ports would be watched or occupied. Any place would do for me. I finally chose a small villa standing alone nearly five miles from any village and thirty miles from any port. To this I ordered them to convey, secretly by night, oil, spare parts, extra torpedoes, storage batteries, reserve periscopes, and everything that I could need for refitting. The little whitewashed villa of a retired confectioner — that was the base from which I operated against England.

The boats lay at Blankenberg, and thither I went. They were working frantically at the defences, and they had only to look seawards to be spurred to fresh exertions. The British fleet was assembling. The ultimatum had not yet expired, but it was evident that a blow would be struck the instant that it did. Four of their aeroplanes, circling at an immense height, were surveying our defences. From the top of the lighthouse I counted thirty battleships and cruisers in the offing, with a number of the trawlers with which in the British service they break through the mine-fields. The approaches were actually sown with two hundred mines, half contact and half observation, but the result showed that they were insufficient to hold off the enemy, since three days later both town and fleet were speedily destroyed.

However, I am not here to tell you the incidents of the war, but to explain my own part in it, which had such a decisive effect upon the result. My first action was to send my four second-class boats away instantly to the point which I had chosen for my base. There they were to wait submerged, lying with negative buoyancy upon the sands in twenty foot of water, and rising only at night. My strict orders were that they were to attempt nothing upon the enemy, however tempting the opportunity. All they had to do was to remain intact and unseen, until they received further orders. Having made this clear to Commander Panza, who had charge of this reserve flotilla, I shook him by the hand and bade him farewell, leaving with him a sheet of notepaper upon which I had explained the tactics to be used and given him certain general principles which he could apply as circumstances demanded.

My whole attention was now given to my own flotilla, which I divided into two divisions, keeping *Iota* and *Kappa* under my own command, while Captain Miriam had *Delta* and *Epsilon*. He was to operate separately in the British Channel, while my station was the Straits of Dover. I made the whole plan of campaign clear to him. Then I saw that each ship was provided with all it could carry. Each had forty tons of heavy oil for surface propulsion and charging the dynamo which supplied the electric engines under water. Each had also eighteen torpedoes as explained and five hundred rounds for the collapsible quick-firing twelve-pounder which we carried on deck, and which, of course, disappeared into a water-tight tank when we were submerged. We carried spare periscopes and a wireless mast, which could be elevated above the conning-tower when necessary. There were provisions for sixteen days for the ten men who manned each craft. Such was the equipment of the four boats which were destined to bring to naught all the navies and armies of Britain. At sundown that day — it was April 10th — we set forth upon our historic voyage.

Miriam had got away in the afternoon, since he had so much farther to go to reach his station. Stephan, of the *Kappa*, started with me; but, of course, we realized that we must work independently, and that from that moment when we shut the sliding hatches of our conning-towers on the still waters of Blankenberg Harbour it was unlikely that we should ever see each other again, though consorts in the same waters. I waved to Stephan from the side of my conning-tower, and he to me. Then I called through the tube to my engineer (our water-tanks were already filled and all kingstons and vents closed) to put her full speed ahead.

Just as we came abreast of the end of the pier and saw the white-capped waves rolling in upon us, I put the horizontal rudder hard down and she slid under water. Through my glass portholes I saw its light green change to a dark blue, while the manometer in front of me indicated twenty feet. I let her go to forty, because I should then be under the warships of the English, though I took the chance of fouling the moorings of our own floating contact mines. Then I brought her on an even keel, and it was music to my ear to hear the gentle, even ticking of my electric engines and to know that I was speeding at twelve miles an hour on my great task.

At that moment, as I stood controlling my levers in my tower, I could have seen, had my cupola been of glass, the vast shadows of the British blockaders hovering above me. I held my course due westward for ninety minutes, and then, by shutting off the electric engine without blowing out the water-tanks, I brought her to the surface. There was a rolling sea and the wind was freshening, so I did not think it safe to keep my hatch open long, for so small is the margin of buoyancy that one must run no risks. But from the crests of the rollers I had a look backwards at Blankenberg, and saw the black funnels and upper works of the enemy's fleet with the lighthouse and the castle behind them, all flushed with the pink glow of the setting sun. Even as I looked there was the boom of a great gun, and then another. I glanced at my watch. It was six o'clock. The time of the ultimatum had expired. We were at war.

There was no craft near us, and our surface speed is nearly twice that of our submerged, so I blew out the tanks and our whale-back came over the surface. All night we were steering south-west, making an average of eighteen knots. At about five in the morning, as I stood alone upon my tiny bridge, I saw, low down in the west, the scattered lights of the Norfolk coast. "Ah, Johnny, Johnny Bull," I said, as I looked at them, "you are going to have your lesson, and I am to be your master. It is I who have been chosen to teach you that one cannot live under artificial conditions and yet act as if they were natural ones. More foresight, Johnny, and less party politics — that is my lesson to you." And then I had a wave of pity, too, when I thought of those vast droves of helpless people, Yorkshire miners, Lancashire spinners, Birmingham metal-workers, the dockers and workers of London, over whose little homes I would bring the shadow of starvation. I seemed to see all those wasted eager hands held out for food, and I, John Sirius, dashing it aside. Ah, well! war is war, and if one is foolish one must pay the price.

Just before daybreak I saw the lights of a considerable town, which must have been Yarmouth, bearing about ten miles west-south-west on our starboard bow. I took her farther out, for it is a sandy, dangerous coast, with many shoals. At five-thirty we were abreast of the Lowestoft lightship. A coastguard was sending up flash signals which faded into a pale twinkle as the white dawn crept over the water. There was a good deal of shipping about, mostly fishing-boats and small coasting craft, with one large steamer hull-down to the west, and a torpedo destroyer between us and the land. It could not harm us, and yet I thought it as well that there should be no word of our presence, so I filled my tanks again and went down to ten feet. I was pleased to find that we got under in one hundred and fifty seconds. The life of one's boat may depend on this when a swift craft comes suddenly upon you.

We were now within a few hours of our cruising ground, so I determined to snatch a rest, leaving Vornal in charge. When he woke me at ten o'clock we were running on the surface, and had reached the Essex coast off the Maplin Sands. With that charming frankness which is one of their characteristics, our friends of England had informed us by their Press that they had put a cordon of torpedo-boats across the Straits of Dover to prevent the passage of submarines, which is about as sensible as to lay a wooden plank across a stream to keep the eels from passing. I knew that Stephan, whose station lay at the western end of the Solent, would have no difficulty in reaching it. My own cruising ground was to be at the mouth of the Thames, and here I was at the very spot with my tiny *Iota*, my eighteen torpedoes, my quick-firing gun, and, above all, a brain that knew what should be done and how to do it.

When I resumed my place in the conning-tower I saw in the periscope (for we had dived) that a lightship was within a few hundred yards of us upon the port bow. Two men were sitting on her bulwarks, but neither of them cast an eye upon the little rod that clove the water so close to them. It was an ideal day for submarine action, with enough ripple upon the surface to make us difficult to detect, and yet smooth enough to give me a clear view. Each of my three periscopes had an angle of sixty degrees so that between them I commanded a complete semi-circle of the horizon. Two British cruisers were steaming north from the Thames within half a mile of me. I could easily have cut them off and attacked them had I allowed myself to be diverted from my great plan. Farther south a destroyer was passing westwards to Sheerness. A dozen small steamers were moving about. None of these were worthy of my notice. Great countries are not provisioned by small steamers. I kept the engines running at the lowest pace which would hold our position under water, and, moving slowly across the estuary, I waited for what must assuredly come.

I had not long to wait. Shortly after one o'clock I perceived in the periscope a cloud of smoke to the south. Half an hour later a large steamer raised her hull, making for the mouth of the Thames. I ordered Vornal to stand by the starboard torpedo-tube, having the other also loaded in case of a miss. Then I advanced slowly, for though the steamer was going very swiftly we could easily cut her off. Presently I laid the *Iota* in a position near which she must pass, and would very gladly have lain to, but could not for fear of rising to the surface. I therefore steered out in the direction from which she was coming. She was a very large ship, fifteen thousand tons at the least, painted black above and red below, with two cream-coloured funnels. She lay so low in the water that it was clear she had a full cargo. At her bows were a cluster of men, some of them looking, I dare say, for the first time at the mother country. How little could they have guessed the welcome that was awaiting them!

On she came with the great plumes of smoke floating from her funnels, and two white waves foaming from her cut-water. She was within a quarter of a mile. My moment had arrived. I signalled full speed ahead and steered straight for her course. My timing was exact. At a hundred yards I gave the signal, and heard the clank and swish of the discharge. At the same instant I put the helm hard down and flew off at an angle. There was a terrific lurch, which came from the distant explosion. For a moment we were almost upon our side. Then, after staggering and trembling, the *Iota* came on an even keel. I stopped the engines, brought her to the surface, and opened the conning-tower, while all my excited crew came crowding to the hatch to know what had happened.

The ship lay within two hundred yards of us, and it was easy to see that she had her death-blow. She was already settling down by the stern. There was a sound of shouting and people were running wildly about her decks. Her name was visible, the *Adela*, of London, bound, as we afterwards learned, from New Zealand with frozen mutton. Strange as it may seem to you, the notion of a submarine had never even now occurred to her people, and all were convinced that they had struck a floating mine. The starboard quarter had been blown in by the explosion, and the ship was sinking rapidly. Their discipline was admirable. We saw boat after boat slip down crowded with people as swiftly and quietly as if it were part of their daily drill. And suddenly, as one of the boats lay off waiting for the others, they caught a glimpse for the first time of my conning-tower so close to them. I saw them shouting and pointing, while the men in the other boats got up to have a better look at us. For my part, I cared nothing, for I took it for granted that they already knew that a submarine had destroyed them. One of them clambered back into the sinking ship. I was sure that he was about to send a wireless message as to our presence. It mattered nothing, since, in any case, it must be known; otherwise I could easily have brought him down with a rifle. As it was, I waved my hand to them, and they waved back to me. War is too big a thing to leave room for personal ill-feeling, but it must be remorseless all the same.

I was still looking at the sinking *Adela* when Vornal, who was beside me, gave a sudden cry of warning and surprise, gripping me by the shoulder and turning my head. There behind us, coming up the fairway, was a huge black vessel with black funnels, flying the well-known house-flag of the P. and O. Company. She was not a mile distant, and I calculated in an instant that even if she had seen us she would not have time to turn and get away before we could reach her. We went straight for her, therefore, keeping awash just as we were. They saw the sinking vessel in front of them and that little dark speck moving over the surface, and they suddenly understood their danger. I saw a number of men rush to the bows, and there was a rattle of rifle-fire. Two bullets were flattened upon our four-inch armour. You might as well try to stop a charging bull with paper pellets as the *Iota* with rifle-fire. I had learned my lesson from the *Adela*, and this time I had the torpedo discharged at a safer distance — two hundred and fifty yards. We caught her amidships and the explosion was tremendous, but we were well outside its area. She sank almost instantaneously. I am sorry for her people, of whom I hear that more than two hundred, including seventy Lascars and forty passengers, were drowned. Yes, I am sorry for them. But when I think of the huge floating granary that went to the bottom, I rejoice as a man does who has carried out that which he plans.

It was a bad afternoon that for the P. and O. Company. The second ship which we destroyed was, as we have since learned, the *Moldavia*, of fifteen thousand tons, one of their finest vessels; but about half-past three we blew up the *Cusco*, of eight thousand, of the same line, also from Eastern ports, and laden with corn. Why she came on in face of the wireless messages which must have warned her of danger, I cannot imagine. The other two steamers which we blew up that day, the *Maid of Athens* (Robson Line) and the *Cormorant*, were neither of them provided with apparatus, and came blindly to their destruction. Both were small boats of from five thousand to seven thousand tons. In the case of the second, I had to rise to the surface and fire six twelve-pound shells under her water-line before she would sink. In each case the crew took to the boats, and so far as I know no casualties occurred.

After that no more steamers came along, nor did I expect them. Warnings must by this time have been flying in all directions. But we had no reason to be dissatisfied with our first day. Between the Maplin Sands and the Nore we had sunk five ships of a total tonnage of about fifty thousand tons. Already the London markets would begin to feel the pinch. And Lloyd's — poor old Lloyd's — what a demented state it would be in! I could imagine the London evening papers and the howling in Fleet Street. We saw the result of our actions, for it was quite laughable to see the torpedo-boats buzzing like angry wasps out of Sheerness in the evening. They were darting in every direction across the estuary, and the aeroplanes and hydroplanes were like flights of crows, black dots against the red western sky. They quartered the whole river mouth, until they discovered us at last. Some sharp-sighted fellow with a telescope on board of a destroyer got a sight of our periscope, and came for us full speed. No doubt he would very gladly have rammed us, even if it had meant his own destruction, but that was not part of our programme at all. I sank her and ran her east-south-east with an occasional rise. Finally we brought her to, not very far from the Kentish coast, and the search-lights of our pursuers were far on the western skyline. There we lay quietly all night, for a submarine at night is nothing more than a very third-rate surface torpedo-boat. Besides, we were all weary and needed rest. Do not forget, you captains of men, when you grease and trim your pumps and compressors and rotators, that the human machine needs some tending also.

I had put up the wireless mast above the conning-tower, and had no difficulty in calling up Captain Stephan. He was lying, he said, off Ventnor and had been unable to reach his station, on account of engine trouble, which he had now set right. Next morning he proposed to block the Southampton approach. He had destroyed one large Indian boat on his way down Channel. We exchanged good wishes. Like myself, he needed rest. I was up at four in the morning, however, and called all hands to overhaul the boat. She was somewhat up by the head, owing to the forward torpedoes having been used, so we trimmed her by opening the forward compensating tank, admitting as much water as the torpedoes had weighed. We also overhauled the starboard air-compressor and one of the periscope motors which had been jarred by the shock of the first explosion. We had hardly got ourselves ship-shape when the morning dawned.

I have no doubt that a good many ships which had taken refuge in the French ports at the first alarm had run across and got safely up the river in the night. Of course I could have attacked them, but I do not care to take risks — and there are always risks for a submarine at night. But one had miscalculated his time, and there she was, just abreast of Warden Point, when the daylight disclosed her to us. In an instant we were after her. It was a near thing, for she was a flier, and could do two miles to our one; but we just reached her as she went swashing by. She saw us at the last moment, for I attacked her awash, since otherwise we could not have had the pace to reach her. She swung away and the first torpedo missed, but the second took her full under the counter. Heavens, what a smash! The whole stern seemed to go aloft. I drew off and watched her sink. She went down in seven minutes, leaving her masts and funnels over the water and a cluster of her people holding on to them. She was the *Virginia*, of the Bibby Line — twelve thousand tons — and laden, like the others, with foodstuffs from the East. The whole surface of the sea was covered with the floating grain. "John Bull will have to take up a hole or two of his belt if this goes on," said Vornal, as we watched the scene.

And it was at that moment that the very worst danger occurred that could befall us. I tremble now when I think how our glorious voyage might have been nipped in the bud. I had freed the hatch of my tower, and was looking at the boats of the *Virginia* with Vornal near me, when there was a swish and a terrific splash in the water beside us, which covered us both with spray. We looked up, and you can imagine our feelings when we saw an aeroplane hovering a few hundred feet above us like a hawk.

With its silencer, it was perfectly noiseless, and had its bomb not fallen into the sea we should never have known what had destroyed us. She was circling round in the hope of dropping a second one, but we shoved on all speed ahead, crammed down the rudders, and vanished into the side of a roller. I kept the deflection indicator falling until I had put fifty good feet of water between the aeroplane and ourselves, for I knew well how deeply they can see under the surface. However, we soon threw her off our track, and when we came to the surface near Margate there was no sign of her, unless she was one of several which we saw hovering over Herne Bay.

There was not a ship in the offing save a few small coasters and little thousand-ton steamers, which were beneath my notice. For several hours I lay submerged with a blank periscope. Then I had an inspiration. Orders had been marconied to every foodship to lie in French waters and dash across after dark. I was as sure of it as if they had been recorded in our own receiver. Well, if they were there, that was where I should be also. I blew out the tanks and rose, for there was no sign of any warship near. They had some good system of signalling from the shore, however, for I had not got to the North Foreland before three destroyers came foaming after me, all converging from different directions. They had about as good a chance of catching me as three spaniels would have of overtaking a porpoise. Out of pure bravado — I know it was very wrong — I waited until they were actually within gunshot. Then I sank and we saw each other no more.

It is, as I have said, a shallow sandy coast, and

submarine navigation is very difficult. The worst mishap that can befall a boat is to bury its nose in the side of a sand-drift and be held there. Such an accident might have been the end of our boat, though with our Fleuss cylinders and electric lamps we should have found no difficulty in getting out at the air-lock and in walking ashore across the bed of the ocean. As it was, however, I was able, thanks to our excellent charts, to keep the channel and so to gain the open straits. There we rose about midday, but, observing a hydroplane at no great distance, we sank again for half an hour. When we came up for the second time, all was peaceful around us, and the English coast was lining the whole western horizon. We kept outside the Goodwins and straight down Channel until we saw a line of black dots in front of us, which I knew to be the Dover-Calais torpedo-boat cordon. When two miles distant we dived and came up again seven miles to the south-west, without one of them dreaming that we had been within thirty feet of their keels.

When we rose, a large steamer flying the German flag was within half a mile of us. It was the North German Lloyd *Altona*, from New York to Bremen. I raised our whole hull and dipped our flag to her. It was amusing to see the amazement of her people at what they must have regarded as our unparalleled impudence in those English-swept waters. They cheered us heartily, and the tricolour flag was dipped in greeting as they went roaring past us. Then I stood in to the French coast.

It was exactly as I had expected. There were three great British steamers lying at anchor in Boulogne outer harbour. They were the *Cæsar*, the *King of the East*, and the *Pathfinder*, none less than ten thousand tons. I suppose they thought they were safe in French waters, but what did I care about three-mile limits and international law! The view of my Government was that England was blockaded, food contraband, and vessels carrying it to be destroyed. The lawyers could argue about it afterwards. My business was to starve the enemy any way I could. Within an hour the three ships were under the waves and the *Iota* was streaming down the Picardy coast, looking for fresh victims. The Channel was covered with English torpedo-boats buzzing and whirling like a cloud of midges. How they thought they could hurt me I cannot imagine, unless by accident I were to come up underneath one of them. More dangerous were the aeroplanes which circled here and there.

The water being calm, I had several times to descend as deep as a hundred feet before I was sure that I was out of their sight. After I had blown up the three ships at Boulogne I saw two aeroplanes flying down Channel, and I knew that they would head off any vessels which were coming up. There was one very large white steamer lying off Havre, but she steamed west before I could reach her. I dare say Stephan or one of the others would get her before long. But those infernal aeroplanes spoiled our sport for that day. Not another steamer did I see, save the never-ending torpedo-boats. I consoled myself with the reflection, however, that no food was passing me on its way to London. That was what I was there for, after all. If I could do it without spending my torpedoes, all the better. Up to date I had fired ten of them and sunk nine steamers, so I had not wasted my weapons. That night I came back to the Kent coast and lay upon the bottom in shallow water near Dungeness.

We were all trimmed and ready at the first break of day, for I expected to catch some ships which had tried to make the Thames in the darkness and had miscalculated their time. Sure enough, there was a great steamer coming up Channel and flying the American flag. It was all the same to me what flag she flew so long as she was engaged in conveying contraband of war to the British Isles. There were no torpedo-boats about at the moment, so I ran out on the surface and fired a shot across her bows. She seemed inclined to go on so I put a second one just above her water-line on her port bow. She stopped then and a very angry man began to gesticulate from the bridge. I ran the *Iota* almost alongside.

"Are you the captain?" I asked.

"What the — " I won't attempt to reproduce his language.

"You have food-stuffs on board?" I said.

"It's an American ship, you blind beetle!" he cried. "Can't you see the flag? It's the *Vermondia*, of Boston."

"Sorry, Captain," I answered. "I have really no time for words. Those shots of mine will bring the torpedo-boats, and I dare say at this very moment your wireless is making trouble for me. Get your people into the boats."

I had to show him I was not bluffing, so I drew off and began putting shells into him just on the water-line. When I had knocked six holes in it he was very busy on his boats. I fired twenty shots altogether, and no torpedo was needed, for she was lying over with a terrible list to port, and presently came right on to her side. There she lay for two or three minutes before she foundered. There were eight boats crammed with people lying round her when she went down. I believe everybody was saved, but I could not wait to inquire. From all quarters the poor old panting, useless war-vessels were hurrying. I filled my tanks, ran her bows under, and came up fifteen miles to the south. Of course, I knew there would be a big row afterwards — as there was — but that did not help the starving crowds round the London bakers, who only saved their skins, poor devils, by explaining to the mob that they had nothing to bake.

By this time I was becoming rather anxious, as you can imagine, to know what was going on in the world and what England was thinking about it all. I ran alongside a fishing-boat, therefore, and ordered them to give up their papers. Unfortunately they had none, except a rag of an evening paper, which was full of nothing but betting news. In a second attempt I came alongside a small yachting party from Eastbourne, who were frightened to death at our sudden appearance out of the depths. From them we were lucky enough to get the London *Courier* of that very morning.

It was interesting reading — so interesting that I had to announce it all to the crew. Of course, you know the British style of headline, which gives you all the news at a glance. It seemed to me that the whole paper was headlines, it was in such a state of excitement. Hardly a word about me and my flotilla. We were on the second page. The first one began something like this: —

CAPTURE OF BLANKENBERG!

* * * * *

destruction of enemy's fleet

* * * * *

burning of town

* * * * *

trawlers destroy mine field
loss of two battleships

* * * * *

is it the end?

Of course, what I had foreseen had occurred. The town was actually occupied by the British. And they thought it was the end! We would see about that.

On the round-the-corner page, at the back of the glorious resonant leaders, there was a little column which read like this: —

HOSTILE SUBMARINES

Several of the enemy's submarines are at sea, and have inflicted some appreciable damage upon our merchant ships. The danger-spots upon Monday and the greater part of Tuesday appear to have been the mouth of the Thames and the western entrance to the Solent. On Monday, between the Nore and Margate, there were sunk five large steamers, the *Adela, Moldavia, Cusco, Cormorant,* and *Maid of Athens,* particulars of which will be found below. Near Ventnor, on the same day, was sunk the *Verulam,* from Bombay. On Tuesday the *Virginia, Cæsar, King of the East,* and *Pathfinder* were destroyed between the Foreland and Boulogne. The latter three were actually lying in French waters, and the most energetic representations have been made by the Government of the Republic. On the same day *The Queen of Sheba, Orontes, Diana,* and *Atalanta* were destroyed near the Needles. Wireless messages have stopped all ingoing cargo-ships from coming up Channel, but unfortunately there is evidence that at least two of the enemy's submarines are in the West. Four cattleships from Dublin to Liverpool were sunk yesterday evening, while three Bristol-bound steamers, *The Hilda, Mercury,* and *Maria Toser,* were blown up in the neighbourhood of Lundy Island. Commerce has, so far as possible, been diverted into safer channels, but in the meantime, however vexatious these incidents may be, and however grievous the loss both to the owners and to Lloyd's, we may console ourselves by the reflection that since a submarine cannot keep the sea for more than ten days without refitting, and since the base has been captured, there must come a speedy term to these depredations."

So much for the *Courier's* account of our proceedings. Another small paragraph was, however, more eloquent: —

"The price of wheat, which stood at thirty-five shillings a week before the declaration of war, was quoted yesterday on the Baltic at fifty-two. Maize has gone from twenty-one to thirty-seven, barley from nineteen to thirty-five, sugar (foreign granulated) from eleven shillings and threepence to nineteen shillings and sixpence."

"Good, my lads!" said I, when I read it to the crew. "I can assure you that those few lines will prove to mean more than the whole page about the Fall of Blankenberg. Now let us get down Channel and send those prices up a little higher."

All traffic had stopped for London — not so bad for the little *Iota* — and we did not see a steamer that was worth a torpedo between Dungeness and the Isle of Wight. There I called Stephan up by wireless, and by seven o'clock we were actually lying side by side in a smooth rolling sea — Hengistbury Head bearing N.N.W. and about five miles distant. The two crews clustered on the whale-backs and shouted their joy at seeing friendly faces once more. Stephan had done extraordinarily well. I had, of course, read in the London paper of his four ships on Tuesday, but he had sunk no fewer than seven since, for many of those which should have come to the Thames had tried to make Southampton. Of the seven, one was of twenty thousand tons, a grain-ship from America, a second was a grain-ship from the Black Sea, and two others were great liners from South Africa. I congratulated Stephan with all my heart upon his splendid achievement. Then as we had been seen by a destroyer which was approaching at a great pace, we both dived, coming up again off the Needles, where we spent the night in company. We could not visit each other, since we had no boat, but we lay so nearly alongside that we were able, Stephan and I, to talk from hatch to hatch and so make our plans.

He had shot away more than half his torpedoes, and so had I, and yet we were very averse from returning to our base so long as our oil held out. I told him of my experience with the Boston steamer, and we mutually agreed to sink the ships by gun-fire in future so far as possible. I remember old Horli saying, "What use is a gun aboard a submarine?" We were about to show. I read the English paper to Stephan by the light of my electric torch, and we both agreed that few ships would now come up the Channel. That sentence about diverting commerce to safer routes could only mean that the ships would go round the North of Ireland and unload at Glasgow. Oh, for two more ships to stop that entrance! Heavens, what *would* England have done against a foe with thirty or forty submarines, since we only needed six instead of four to complete her destruction! After much talk we decided that the best plan would be that I should dispatch a cipher telegram next morning from a French port to tell them to send the four second-rate boats to cruise off the North of Ireland and West of Scotland. Then when I had done this I should move down Channel with Stephan and operate at the mouth, while the other two boats could work in the Irish Sea. Having made these plans, I set off across the Channel in the early morning, reaching the small village of Etretat, in Brittany. There I got off my telegram and then laid my course for Falmouth, passing under the keels of two British cruisers which were making eagerly for Etretat, having heard by wireless that we were there.

Half-way down Channel we had trouble with a short circuit in our electric engines, and were compelled to run on the surface for several hours while we replaced one of the cam-shafts and renewed some washers. It was a ticklish time, for had a torpedo-boat come upon us we could not have dived. The perfect submarine of the future will surely have some alternative engines for such an emergency. However by the skill of Engineer Morro, we got things going once more. All the time we lay there I saw a hydroplane floating between us and the British coast. I can understand how a mouse feels when it is in a tuft of grass and sees a hawk high up in the heavens. However, all went well; the mouse became a water-rat, it wagged its tail in derision at the poor blind old hawk, and it dived down into a nice safe green, quiet world where there was nothing to injure it.

It was on the Wednesday night that the *Iota* crossed to Etretat. It was Friday afternoon before we had reached our new cruising ground. Only one large steamer did I see upon our way. The terror we had caused had cleared the Channel. This big boat had a clever captain on board. His tactics were excellent and took him in safety to the Thames. He came zigzagging up Channel at twenty-five knots, shooting off from his course at all sorts of unexpected angles. With our slow pace we could not catch him, nor could we calculate his line so as to cut him off. Of course, he had never seen us, but he judged, and judged rightly, that wherever we were those were the tactics by which he had the best chance of getting past. He deserved his success.

But, of course, it is only in a wide Channel that such things can be done. Had I met him in the mouth of the Thames there would have been a different story to tell. As I approached Falmouth I destroyed a three-thousand-ton boat from Cork, laden with butter and cheese. It was my only success for three days.

That night (Friday, April 16th) I called up Stephan, but received no reply. As I was within a few miles of our rendezvous, and as he would not be cruising after dark, I was puzzled to account for his silence. I could only imagine that his wireless was deranged. But, alas!

I was soon to find the true reason from a copy of the *Western Morning News*, which I obtained from a Brixham trawler. The *Kappa*, with her gallant commander and crew, were at the bottom of the English Channel.

It appeared from this account that after I had parted from him he had met and sunk no fewer than five vessels. I gathered these to be his work, since all of them were by gun-fire, and all were on the south coast of Dorset or Devon. How he met his fate was stated in a short telegram which was headed "Sinking of a Hostile Submarine." It was marked "Falmouth," and ran thus: —

The P. and O. mail steamer *Macedonia* came into this port last night with five shell holes between wind and water. She reports having been attacked by a hostile submarine ten miles to the south-east of the Lizard. Instead of using her torpedoes, the submarine for some reason approached from the surface and fired five shots from a semi-automatic twelve-pounder gun. She was evidently under the impression that the *Macedonia* was unarmed. As a matter of fact, being warned of the presence of submarines in the Channel, the *Macedonia* had mounted her armament as an auxiliary cruiser. She opened fire with two quick-firers and blew away the conning-tower of the submarine. It is probable that the shells went right through her, as she sank at once with her hatches open. The *Macedonia* was only kept afloat by her pumps.

Such was the end of the *Kappa*, and my gallant friend, Commander Stephan. His best epitaph was in a corner of the same paper, and was headed "Mark Lane." It ran: —

"Wheat (average) 66, maize 48, barley 50."

Well, if Stephan was gone there was the more need for me to show energy. My plans were quickly taken, but they were comprehensive. All that day (Saturday) I passed down the Cornish coast and round Land's End, getting two steamers on the way. I had learned from Stephan's fate that it was better to torpedo the large craft, but I was aware that the auxiliary cruisers of the British Government were all over ten thousand tons, so that for all ships under that size it was safe to use my gun. Both these craft, the *Yelland* and the *Playboy* — the latter an American ship — were perfectly harmless, so I came up within a hundred yards of them and speedily sank them, after allowing their people to get into boats. Some other steamers lay farther out, but I was so eager to make my new arrangements that I did not go out of my course to molest them. Just before sunset, however, so magnificent a prey came within my radius of action that I could not possibly refuse her. No sailor could fail to recognize that glorious monarch of the sea, with her four cream funnels tipped with black, her huge black sides, her red bilges, and her high white top-hamper, roaring up Channel at twenty-three knots, and carrying her forty-five thousand tons as lightly as if she were a five-ton motor-boat. It was the queenly *Olympic*, of the White Star — once the largest and still the comeliest of liners. What a picture she made, with the blue Cornish sea creaming round her giant fore-foot, and the pink western sky with one evening star forming the background to her noble lines.

She was about five miles off when we dived to cut her off. My calculation was exact. As we came abreast we loosed our torpedo and struck her fair. We swirled round with the concussion of the water. I saw her in my periscope list over on her side, and I knew that she had her death-blow. She settled down slowly, and there was plenty of time to save her people. The sea was dotted with her boats. When I got about three miles off I rose to the surface, and the whole crew clustered up to see the wonderful sight. She dived bows foremost, and there was a terrific explosion, which sent one of the funnels into the air. I suppose we should have cheered — somehow, none of us felt like cheering. We were all keen sailors, and it went to our hearts to see such a ship go down like a broken eggshell. I gave a gruff order, and all were at their posts again while we headed north-west. Once round the Land's End I called up my two consorts, and we met next day at Hartland Point, the south end of Bideford Bay. For the moment the Channel was clear, but the English could not know it, and I reckoned that the loss of the *Olympic* would stop all ships for a day or two at least.

Having assembled the *Delta* and *Epsilon*, one on each side of me, I received the report from Miriam and Var, the respective commanders. Each had expended twelve torpedoes, and between them they had sunk twenty-two steamers. One man had been killed by the machinery on board of the *Delta*, and two had been burned by the ignition of some oil on the *Epsilon*. I took these injured men on board, and I gave each of the boats one of my crew. I also divided my spare oil, my provisions, and my torpedoes among them, though we had the greatest possible difficulty in those crank vessels in transferring them from one to the other. However, by ten o'clock it was done, and the two vessels were in condition to keep the sea for another ten days. For my part, with only two torpedoes left, I headed north up the Irish Sea. One of my torpedoes I expended that evening upon a cattle-ship making for Milford Haven. Late at night, being abreast of Holyhead, I called upon my four northern boats, but without reply. Their Marconi range is very limited. About three in the afternoon of the next day I had a feeble answer. It was a great relief to me to find that my telegraphic instructions had reached them and that they were on their station. Before evening we all assembled in the lee of

Sanda Island, in the Mull of Kintyre. I felt an admiral indeed when I saw my five whale-backs all in a row. Panza's report was excellent. They had come round by the Pentland Firth and reached their cruising ground on the fourth day. Already they had destroyed twenty vessels without any mishap. I ordered the *Beta* to divide her oil and torpedoes among the other three, so that they were in good condition to continue their cruise. Then the *Beta* and I headed for home, reaching our base upon Sunday, April 25th. Off Cape Wrath I picked up a paper from a small schooner.

"Wheat, 84; Maize, 60; Barley, 62." What were battles and bombardments compared to that!

The whole coast of Norland was closely blockaded by cordon within cordon, and every port, even the smallest, held by the British. But why should they suspect my modest confectioner's villa more than any other of the ten thousand houses that face the sea? I was glad when I picked up its homely white front in my periscope. That night I landed and found my stores intact. Before morning the *Beta* reported itself, for we had the windows lit as a guide.

It is not for me to recount the messages which I found waiting for me at my humble headquarters. They shall ever remain as the patents of nobility of my family. Among others was that never-to-be-forgotten salutation from my King. He desired me to present myself at Hauptville, but for once I took it upon myself to disobey his commands. It took me two days — or rather two nights, for we sank ourselves during the daylight hours — to get all our stores on board, but my presence was needful every minute of the time. On the third morning, at four o'clock, the *Beta* and my own little flagship were at sea once more, bound for our original station off the mouth of the Thames.

I had no time to read our papers whilst I was refitting, but I gathered the news after we got under way. The British occupied all our ports, but otherwise we had not suffered at all, since we have excellent railway communications with Europe. Prices had altered little, and our industries continued as before. There was talk of a British invasion, but this I knew to be absolute nonsense, for the British must have learned by this time that it would be sheer murder to send transports full of soldiers to sea in the face of submarines. When they have a tunnel they can use their fine expeditionary force upon the Continent, but until then it might just as well not exist so far as Europe is concerned. My own country, therefore, was in good case and had nothing to fear. Great Britain, however, was already feeling my grip upon her throat. As in normal times four-fifths of her food is imported, prices were rising by leaps and bounds. The supplies in the country were beginning to show signs of depletion, while little was coming in to replace it. The insurances at Lloyd's had risen to a figure which made the price of the food prohibitive to the mass of the people by the time it had reached the market. The loaf, which, under ordinary circumstances stood at fivepence, was already at one and twopence. Beef was three shillings and fourpence a pound, and mutton two shillings and ninepence. Everything else was in proportion. The

Government had acted with energy and offered a big bounty for corn to be planted at once. It could only be reaped five months hence, however, and long before then, as the papers pointed out, half the island would be dead from starvation. Strong appeals had been made to the patriotism of the people, and they were assured that the interference with trade was temporary, and that with a little patience all would be well. But already there was a marked rise in the death-rate, especially among children, who suffered from want of milk, the cattle being slaughtered for food. There was serious rioting in the Lanarkshire coalfields and in the Midlands, together with a Socialistic upheaval in the East of London, which had assumed the proportions of a civil war. Already there were responsible papers which declared that England was in an impossible position, and that an immediate peace was necessary to prevent one of the greatest tragedies in history. It was my task now to prove to them that they were right.

It was May 2nd when I found myself back at the Maplin Sands to the north of the estuary of the Thames. The *Beta* was sent on to the Solent to block it and take the place of the lamented *Kappa*. And now I was throttling Britain indeed — London, Southampton, the Bristol Channel, Liverpool, the North Channel, the Glasgow approaches, each was guarded by my boats. Great liners were, as we learned afterwards, pouring their supplies into Galway and the West of Ireland, where provisions were cheaper than has ever been known. Tens of thousands were embarking from Britain for Ireland in order to save themselves from starvation. But you cannot transplant a whole dense population. The main body of the people, by the middle of May, were actually starving. At that date wheat was at a hundred, maize and barley at eighty. Even the most obstinate had begun to see that the situation could not possibly continue.

In the great towns starving crowds clamoured for bread before the municipal offices, and public officials everywhere were attacked and often murdered by frantic mobs, composed largely of desperate women who had seen their infants perish before their eyes. In the country, roots, bark, and weeds of every sort were used as food. In London the private mansions of Ministers were guarded by strong pickets of soldiers, while a battalion of Guards was camped permanently round the Houses of Parliament. The lives of the Prime Minister and of the Foreign Secretary were continually threatened and occasionally attempted. Yet the Government had entered upon the war with the full assent of every party in the State. The true culprits were those, be they politicians or journalists, who had not the foresight to understand that unless Britain grew her own supplies, or unless by means of a tunnel she had some way of conveying them into the island, all her mighty expenditure upon her army and her fleet was a mere waste of money so long as her antagonists had a few submarines and men who could use them. England has often been stupid, but has got off scotfree. This time she was stupid and had to pay the price. You can't expect Luck to be your saviour always.

It would be a mere repetition of what I have already described if I were to recount all our proceedings during that first ten days after I resumed my station. During my absence the ships had taken heart and had begun to come up again. In the first day I got four. After that I had to go farther afield, and again I picked up several in French waters. Once I had a narrow escape through one of my kingston valves getting some grit into it and refusing to act when I was below the surface. Our margin of buoyancy just carried us through. By the end of that week the Channel was clear again, and both *Beta* and my own boat were down West once more. There we had encouraging messages from our Bristol consort, who in turn had heard from *Delta* at Liverpool. Our task was completely done. We could not prevent all food from passing into the British Islands, but at least we had raised what did get in to a price which put it far beyond the means of the penniless, workless multitudes. In vain Government commandeered it all and doled it out as a general feeds the garrison of a fortress. The task was too great — the responsibility too horrible. Even the proud and stubborn English could not face it any longer.

I remember well how the news came to me. I was lying at the time off Selsey Bill when I saw a small war-vessel coming down Channel. It had never been my policy to attack any vessel coming *down*. My torpedoes and even my shells were too precious for that. I could not help being attracted, however, by the movements of this ship, which came slowly zigzagging in my direction.

"Looking for me," thought I. "What on earth does the foolish thing hope to do if she could find me?"

I was lying awash at the time and got ready to go below in case she should come for me. But at that moment — she was about half a mile away — she turned her quarter, and there to my amazement was the red flag with the blue circle, our own beloved flag, flying from her peak. For a moment I thought that this was some clever dodge of the enemy to tempt me within range. I snatched up my glasses and called on Vornal. Then we both recognized the vessel. It was the *Juno*, the only one left intact of our own cruisers. What could she be doing flying the flag in the enemy's waters? Then I understood it, and turning to Vornal, we threw ourselves into each other's arms. It could only mean an armistice — or peace!

And it was peace. We learned the glad news when we had risen alongside the *Juno*, and the ringing cheers which greeted us had at last died away. Our orders were to report ourselves at once at Blankenberg. Then she passed on down Channel to collect the others. We returned to port upon the surface, steaming through the whole British fleet as we passed up the North Sea. The crews clustered thick along the sides of the vessels to watch us. I can see now their sullen, angry faces. Many shook their fists and cursed us as we went by. It was not that we had damaged them — I will do them the justice to say that the English, as the old Boer War has proved, bear no resentment against a brave enemy — but that they thought us cowardly to attack merchant ships and avoid the warships. It is like the Arabs who think that a flank attack is a mean, unmanly device. War is not a big game, my English friends. It is a desperate business to gain the upper hand, and one must use one's brain in order to find the weak spot of one's enemy. It is not fair to blame me if I have found yours. It was my duty. Perhaps those officers and sailors who scowled at the little *Iota* that May morning have by this time done me justice when the first bitterness of undeserved defeat was passed.

Let others describe my entrance into Blankenberg; the mad enthusiasm of the crowds, and the magnificent public reception of each successive boat as it arrived. Surely the men deserved the grant made them by the State which has enabled each of them to be independent for life. As a feat of endurance, that long residence in such a state of mental tension in cramped quarters, breathing an unnatural atmosphere, will long remain as a record. The country may well be proud of such sailors.

The terms of peace were not made onerous, for we were in no condition to make Great Britain our permanent enemy. We knew well that we had won the war by circumstances which would never be allowed to occur again, and that in a few years the Island Power would be as strong as ever — stronger, perhaps — for the lesson that she had learned. It would be madness to provoke such an antagonist. A mutual salute of flags was arranged, the Colonial boundary was adjusted by arbitration, and we claimed no indemnity beyond an undertaking on the part of Britain that she would pay any damages which an International Court might award to France or to the United States for injury received through the operations of our submarines. So ended the war!

Of course, England will not be caught napping in such a fashion again! Her foolish blindness is partly explained by her delusion that her enemy would not torpedo merchant vessels. Common sense should have told her that her enemy will play the game that suits them best — that they will not inquire what they may do, but they will do it first and talk about it afterwards. The opinion of the whole world now is that if a blockade were proclaimed one may do what one can with those who try to break it, and that it was as reasonable to prevent food from reaching England in war time as it is for a besieger to prevent the victualling of a beleaguered fortress.

I cannot end this account better than by quoting the first few paragraphs of a leader in the *Times*, which appeared shortly after the declaration of peace. It may be taken to epitomize the saner public opinion of England upon the meaning and lessons of the episode.

"In all this miserable business," said the writer, "which has cost us the loss of a considerable portion of our merchant fleet and more than fifty thousand civilian lives, there is just one consolation to be found. It lies in the fact that our temporary conqueror is a Power which is not strong enough to reap the fruits of her victory. Had we endured this humiliation at the hands of any of the first-class Powers it would certainly have entailed the loss of all our Crown Colonies and tropical possessions, besides the payment of a huge indemnity. We were absolutely at the feet of our conqueror and had no possible alternative but to submit to her terms, however onerous. Norland has had the good sense to understand that she must not abuse her temporary advantage, and has been generous in her dealings. In the grip of any other Power we should have ceased to exist as an Empire.

"Even now we are not out of the wood. Some one may maliciously pick a quarrel with us before we get our house in order, and use the easy weapon which has been demonstrated. It is to meet such a contingency that the Government has rushed enormous stores of food at the public expense into the country. In a very few months the new harvest will have appeared. On the whole we can face the immediate future without undue depression, though there remain some causes for anxiety. These will no doubt be energetically handled by this new and efficient Government, which has taken the place of those discredited politicians who led us into a war without having foreseen how helpless we were against an obvious form of attack.

"Already the lines of our reconstruction are evident. The first and most important is that our Party men realize that there is something more vital than their academic disputes about Free Trade or Protection, and that all theory must give way to the fact that a country is in an artificial and dangerous condition if she does not produce within her own borders sufficient food to at least keep life in her population. Whether this should be brought about by a tax upon foreign foodstuffs, or by a bounty upon home products, or by a combination of the two, is now under discussion. But all Parties are combined upon the principle, and, though it will undoubtedly entail either a rise in prices or a deterioration in quality in the food of the working-classes, they will at least be insured against so terrible a visitation as that which is fresh in our memories. At any rate, we have got past the stage of argument. It *must* be so. The increased prosperity of the farming interest, and, as we will hope, the cessation of agricultural emigration, will be benefits to be counted against the obvious disadvantages.

"The second lesson is the immediate construction of not one but two double-lined railways under the Channel. We stand in a white sheet over the matter, since the project has always been discouraged in these columns, but we are prepared to admit that had such railway communication been combined with adequate arrangements for forwarding supplies from Marseilles, we should have avoided our recent surrender. We still insist that we cannot trust entirely to a tunnel, since our enemy might have allies in the Mediterranean; but in a single contest with any Power of the North of Europe it would certainly be of inestimable benefit. There may be dangers attendant upon the existence of a tunnel, but it must now be admitted that they are trivial compared to those which come from its absence. As to the building of large fleets of merchant submarines for the carriage of food, that is a new departure which will be an additional insurance against the danger which has left so dark a page in the history of our country."

II. ONE CROWDED HOUR

The place was the Eastbourne-Tunbridge road, not very far from the Cross in Hand — a lonely stretch, with a heath running upon either side. The time was half-past eleven upon a Sunday night in the late summer. A motor was passing slowly down the road.

It was a long, lean Rolls-Royce, running smoothly with a gentle purring of the engine. Through the two vivid circles cast by the electric head-lights the waving grass fringes and clumps of heather streamed swiftly like some golden cinematograph, leaving a blacker darkness behind and around them. One ruby-red spot shone upon the road, but no number-plate was visible within the dim ruddy halo of the tail-lamp which cast it. The car was open and of a tourist type, but even in that obscure light, for the night was moonless, an observer could hardly fail to have noticed a curious indefiniteness in its lines. As it slid into and across the broad stream of light from an open cottage door the reason could be seen. The body was hung with a singular loose arrangement of brown holland. Even the long black bonnet was banded with some close-drawn drapery.

The solitary man who drove this curious car was broad and burly. He sat hunched up over his steering-wheel, with the brim of a Tyrolean hat drawn down over his eyes. The red end of a cigarette smouldered under the black shadow thrown by the headgear. A dark ulster of some frieze-like material was turned up in the collar until it covered his ears.

His neck was pushed forward from his rounded shoulders, and he seemed, as the car now slid noiselessly down the long, sloping road, with the clutch disengaged and the engine running free, to be peering ahead of him through the darkness in search of some eagerly-expected object.

The distant toot of a motor-horn came faintly from some point far to the south of him. On such a night, at such a place, all traffic must be from south to north when the current of London week-enders sweeps back from the watering-place to the capital — from pleasure to duty. The man sat straight and listened intently. Yes, there it was again, and certainly to the south of him. His face was over the wheel and his eyes strained through the darkness. Then suddenly he spat out his cigarette and gave a sharp intake of the breath. Far away down the road two little yellow points had rounded a curve. They vanished into a dip, shot upwards once more, and then vanished again. The inert man in the draped car woke suddenly into intense life. From his pocket he pulled a mask of dark cloth, which he fastened securely across his face, adjusting it carefully that his sight might be unimpeded. For an instant he uncovered an acetylene hand-lantern, took a hasty glance at his own preparations, and laid it beside a Mauser pistol upon the seat alongside him. Then, twitching his hat down lower than ever, he released his clutch and slid downward his gear-lever. With a chuckle and shudder the long, black machine sprang forward, and shot with a soft sigh from her powerful engines down the sloping gradient. The driver stooped and switched off his electric head-lights.

Only a dim grey swathe cut through the black heath indicated the line of his road. From in front there came presently a confused puffing and rattling and clanging as the oncoming car breasted the slope. It coughed and spluttered on a powerful, old-fashioned low gear, while its engine throbbed like a weary heart. The yellow, glaring lights dipped for the last time into a switchback curve. When they reappeared over the crest the two cars were within thirty yards of each other. The dark one darted across the road and barred the other's passage, while a warning acetylene lamp was waved in the air. With a jarring of brakes the noisy new-comer was brought to a halt.

"I say," cried an aggrieved voice, "'pon my soul, you know, we might have had an accident. Why the devil don't you keep your head-lights on? I never saw you till I nearly burst my radiators on you!"

The acetylene lamp, held forward, discovered a very angry young man, blue-eyed, yellow-moustached, and florid, sitting alone at the wheel of an antiquated twelve-horse Wolseley. Suddenly the aggrieved look upon his flushed face changed to one of absolute bewilderment. The driver in the dark car had sprung out of the seat, a black, long-barrelled, wicked-looking pistol was poked in the traveller's face, and behind the further sights of it was a circle of black cloth with two deadly eyes looking from as many slits.

"Hands up!" said a quick, stern voice. "Hands up! or, by the Lord — "

The young man was as brave as his neighbours, but the hands went up all the same.

"Get down!" said his assailant, curtly.

The young man stepped forth into the road, followed closely by the covering lantern and pistol. Once he made as if he would drop his hands, but a short, stern word jerked them up again.

"I say, look here, this is rather out o' date, ain't it?" said the traveller. "I expect you're joking — what?"

"Your watch," said the man behind the Mauser pistol.

"You can't really mean it!"

"Your watch, I say!"

"Well, take it, if you must. It's only plated, anyhow. You're two centuries out in time, or a few thousand miles longitude. The bush is your mark — or America. You don't seem in the picture on a Sussex road."

"Purse," said the man. There was something very compelling in his voice and methods. The purse was handed over.

"Any rings?"

"Don't wear 'em."

"Stand there! Don't move!"

The highwayman passed his victim and threw open the bonnet of the Wolseley. His hand, with a pair of steel pliers, was thrust deep into the works.

There was the snap of a parting wire.

"Hang it all, don't crock my car!" cried the traveller.

He turned, but quick as a flash the pistol was at his head once more. And yet even in that flash, whilst the robber whisked round from the broken circuit, something had caught the young man's eye which made him gasp and start. He opened his mouth as if about to shout some words. Then with an evident effort he restrained himself.

"Get in," said the highwayman.

The traveller climbed back to his seat.

"What is your name?"

"Ronald Barker. What's yours?"

The masked man ignored the impertinence.

"Where do you live?" he asked.

"My cards are in my purse. Take one."

The highwayman sprang into his car, the engine of which had hissed and whispered in gentle accompaniment to the interview. With a clash he threw back his side-brake, flung in his gears, twirled the wheel hard round, and cleared the motionless Wolseley. A minute later he was gliding swiftly, with all his lights' gleaming, some half-mile southward on the road, while Mr. Ronald Barker, a side-lamp in his hand, was rummaging furiously among the odds and ends of his repair-box for a strand of wire which would connect up his electricity and set him on his way once more.

When he had placed a safe distance between himself and his victim, the adventurer eased up, took his booty from his pocket, replaced the watch, opened the purse, and counted out the money. Seven shillings constituted the miserable spoil. The poor result of his efforts seemed to amuse rather than annoy him, for he chuckled as he held the two half-crowns and the florin in the glare of his lantern. Then suddenly his manner changed. He thrust the thin purse back into his pocket, released his brake, and shot onwards with the same tense bearing with which he had started upon his adventure. The lights of another car were coming down the road.

On this occasion the methods of the highway-man were less furtive. Experience had clearly given him confidence. With lights still blazing, he ran towards the new-comers, and, halting in the middle of the road, summoned them to stop. From the point of view of the astonished travellers the result was sufficiently impressive. They saw in the glare of their own head-lights two glowing discs on either side of the long, black-muzzled snout of a high-power car, and above the masked face and menacing figure of its solitary driver. In the golden circle thrown by the rover there stood an elegant, open-topped, twenty-horse Humber, with an undersized and very astonished chauffeur blinking from under his peaked cap. From behind the wind-screen the veil-bound hats and wondering faces of two very pretty young women protruded, one upon either side, and a little crescendo of frightened squeaks announced the acute emotion of one of them. The other was cooler and more critical.

"Don't give it away, Hilda," she whispered. "Do shut up, and don't be such a silly. It's Bertie or one of the boys playing it on us."

"No, no! It's the real thing, Flossie. It's a robber, sure enough. Oh, my goodness, whatever shall we do?"

"What an 'ad.'!" cried the other. "Oh, what a glorious 'ad.'! Too late now for the mornings, but they'll have it in every evening paper, sure."

"What's it going to cost?" groaned the other. "Oh, Flossie, Flossie, I'm sure I'm going to faint! Don't you think if we both screamed together we could do some good? Isn't he too awful with that black thing over his face? Oh, dear, oh, dear! He's killing poor little Alf!"

The proceedings of the robber were indeed somewhat alarming. Springing down from his car, he had pulled the chauffeur out of his seat by the scruff of his neck. The sight of the Mauser had cut short all remonstrance, and under its compulsion the little man had pulled open the bonnet and extracted the sparking plugs. Having thus secured the immobility of his capture, the masked man walked forward, lantern in hand, to the side of the car. He had laid aside the gruff sternness with which he had treated Mr. Ronald Barker, and his voice and manner were gentle, though determined. He even raised his hat as a prelude to his address.

"I am sorry to inconvenience you, ladies," said he, and his voice had gone up several notes since the previous interview. "May I ask who you are?"

Miss Hilda was beyond coherent speech, but Miss Flossie was of a sterner mould.

"This is a pretty business," said she. "What right have you to stop us on the public road, I should like to know?"

"My time is short," said the robber, in a sterner voice. "I must ask you to answer my question."

"Tell him, Flossie! For goodness' sake be nice to him!" cried Hilda.

"Well, we're from the Gaiety Theatre, London, if you want to know," said the young lady. "Perhaps you've heard of Miss Flossie Thornton and Miss Hilda Mannering? We've been playing a week at the Royal at Eastbourne, and took a Sunday off to ourselves. So now you know!"

"I must ask you for your purses and for your jewellery."

Both ladies set up shrill expostulations, but they found, as Mr. Ronald Barker had done, that there was something quietly compelling in this man's methods. In a very few minutes they had handed over their purses, and a pile of glittering rings, bangles, brooches, and chains was lying upon the front seat of the car. The diamonds glowed and shimmered like little electric points in the light of the lantern. He picked up the glittering tangle and weighed it in his hand.

"Anything you particularly value?" he asked the ladies; but Miss Flossie was in no humour for concessions.

"Don't come the Claude Duval over us," said she. "Take the lot or leave the lot. We don't want bits of our own given back to us."

"Except just Billy's necklace!" cried Hilda, and snatched at a little rope of pearls. The robber bowed, and released his hold of it.

"Anything else?"

The valiant Flossie began suddenly to cry. Hilda did the same. The effect upon the robber was surprising. He threw the whole heap of jewellery into the nearest lap.

"There! there! Take it!" he said. "It's trumpery stuff, anyhow. It's worth something to you, and nothing to me."

Tears changed in a moment to smiles.

"You're welcome to the purses. The 'ad.' is worth ten times the money. But what a funny way of getting a living nowadays! Aren't you afraid of being caught? It's all so wonderful, like a scene from a comedy."

"It may be a tragedy," said the robber.

"Oh, I hope not — I'm sure I hope not!" cried the two ladies of the drama.

But the robber was in no mood for further conversation. Far away down the road tiny points of light had appeared. Fresh business was coming to him, and he must not mix his cases. Disengaging his machine, he raised his hat, and slipped off to meet this new arrival, while Miss Flossie and Miss Hilda leaned out of their derelict car, still palpitating from their adventure, and watched the red gleam of the tail-light until it merged into the darkness.

This time there was every sign of a rich prize. Behind its four grand lamps set in a broad frame of glittering brasswork the magnificent sixty-horse Daimler breasted the slope with the low, deep, even snore which proclaimed its enormous latent strength. Like some rich-laden, high-pooped Spanish galleon, she kept her course until the prowling craft ahead of her swept across her bows and brought her to a sudden halt. An angry face, red, blotched, and evil, shot out of the open window of the closed limousine. The robber was aware of a high, bald forehead, gross pendulous cheeks, and two little crafty eyes which gleamed between creases of fat.

"Out of my way, sir! Out of my way this instant!" cried a rasping voice. "Drive over him, Hearn! Get down and pull him off the seat. The fellow's drunk — he's drunk I say!"

Up to this point the proceedings of the modern highwayman might have passed as gentle. Now they turned in an instant to savagery. The chauffeur, a burly, capable fellow, incited by that raucous voice behind him, sprang from the car and seized the advancing robber by the throat. The latter hit out with the butt-end of his pistol, and the man dropped groaning on the road. Stepping over his prostrate body the adventurer pulled open the door, seized the stout occupant savagely by the ear, and dragged him bellowing on to the highway. Then, very deliberately, he struck him twice across the face with his open hand. The blows rang out like pistol-shots in the silence of the night. The fat traveller turned a ghastly colour and fell back half senseless against the side of the limousine. The robber dragged open his coat, wrenched away the heavy gold watch-chain with all that it held, plucked out the great diamond pin that sparkled in the black satin tie, dragged off four rings — not one of which could have cost less than three figures and finally tore from his inner pocket a bulky leather note-book. All this property he transferred to his own black overcoat, and added to it the man's pearl cuff-links, and even the golden stud which held his collar. Having made sure that there was nothing else to take, the robber flashed his lantern upon the prostrate chauffeur, and satisfied himself that he was stunned and not dead. Then, returning to the master, he proceeded very deliberately to tear all his clothes from his body with a ferocious energy which set his victim whimpering and writhing in imminent expectation of murder.

Whatever his tormentor's intention may have been, it was very effectually frustrated. A sound made him turn his head, and there, no very great distance off, were the lights of a car coming swiftly from the north. Such a car must have already passed the wreckage which this pirate had left behind him. It was following his track with a deliberate purpose, and might be crammed with every county constable of the district.

The adventurer had no time to lose. He darted from his bedraggled victim, sprang into his own seat, and with his foot on the accelerator shot swiftly off down the road. Some way down there was a narrow side lane, and into this the fugitive turned, cracking on his high speed and leaving a good five miles between him and any pursuer before he ventured to stop. Then, in a quiet corner, he counted over his booty of the evening — the paltry plunder of Mr. Ronald Barker, the rather better-furnished purses of the actresses, which contained four pounds between them, and, finally, the gorgeous jewellery and well-filled note-book of the plutocrat upon the Daimler. Five notes of fifty pounds, four of ten, fifteen sovereigns, and a number of valuable papers made up a most noble haul. It was clearly enough for one night's work. The adventurer replaced all his ill-gotten gains in his pocket, and, lighting a cigarette, set forth upon his way with the air of a man who has no further care upon his mind.

* * * * *

It was on the Monday morning following upon this eventful evening that Sir Henry Hailworthy, of Walcot Old Place, having finished his breakfast in a leisurely fashion, strolled down to his study with the intention of writing a few letters before setting forth to take his place upon the county bench. Sir Henry was a Deputy-Lieutenant of the county; he was a baronet of ancient blood; he was a magistrate of ten years' standing; and he was famous above all as the breeder of many a good horse and the most desperate rider in all the Weald country. A tall, upstanding man, with a strong, clean-shaven face, heavy black eyebrows, and a square, resolute jaw, he was one whom it was better to call friend than foe. Though nearly fifty years of age, he bore no sign of having passed his youth, save that Nature, in one of her freakish moods, had planted one little feather of white hair above his right ear, making the rest of his thick black curls the darker by contrast. He was in thoughtful mood this morning, for having lit his pipe he sat at his desk with his blank note-paper in front of him, lost in a deep reverie.

Suddenly his thoughts were brought back to the present. From behind the laurels of the curving drive there came a low, clanking sound, which swelled into the clatter and jingle of an ancient car. Then from round the corner there swung an old-fashioned Wolseley, with a fresh-complexioned, yellow-moustached young man at the wheel. Sir Henry sprang to his feet at the sight, and then sat down once more. He rose again as a minute later the footman announced Mr. Ronald Barker. It was an early visit, but Barker was Sir Henry's intimate friend. As each was a fine shot, horseman, and billiard-player, there was much in common between the two men, and the younger (and poorer) was in the habit of spending at least two evenings a week at Walcot Old Place. Therefore, Sir Henry advanced cordially with outstretched hand to welcome him.

"You're an early bird this morning," said he. "What's up? If you are going over to Lewes we could motor together."

But the younger man's demeanour was peculiar and ungracious. He disregarded the hand which was held out to him, and he stood pulling at his own long moustache and staring with troubled, questioning eyes at the county magistrate.

"Well, what's the matter?" asked the latter.

Still the young man did not speak. He was clearly on the edge of an interview which he found it most difficult to open. His host grew impatient.

"You don't seem yourself this morning. What on earth is the matter? Anything upset you?"

"Yes," said Ronald Barker, with emphasis.

"What has?"

"*You* have."

Sir Henry smiled. "Sit down, my dear fellow. If you have any grievance against me, let me hear it."

Barker sat down. He seemed to be gathering himself for a reproach. When it did come it was like a bullet from a gun.

"Why did you rob me last night?"

The magistrate was a man of iron nerve. He showed neither surprise nor resentment. Not a muscle twitched upon his calm, set face.

"Why do you say that I robbed you last night?"

"A big, tall fellow in a motor-car stopped me on the Mayfield road. He poked a pistol in my face and took my purse and my watch. Sir Henry, that man was you."

The magistrate smiled.

"Am I the only big, tall man in the district? Am I the only man with a motor-car?"

"Do you think I couldn't tell a Rolls-Royce

when I see it — I, who spend half my life on a car and the other half under it? Who has a Rolls-Royce about here except you?"

"My dear Barker, don't you think that such a modern highwayman as you describe would be more likely to operate outside his own district? How many hundred Rolls-Royces are there in the South of England?"

"No, it won't do, Sir Henry — it won't do! Even your voice, though you sunk it a few notes, was familiar enough to me. But hang it, man! What did you do it *for*? That's what gets over me. That you should stick up me, one of your closest friends, a man that worked himself to the bone when you stood for the division — and all for the sake of a Brummagem watch and a few shillings — is simply incredible."

"Simply incredible," repeated the magistrate, with a smile.

"And then those actresses, poor little devils, who have to earn all they get. I followed you down the road, you see. That was a dirty trick, if ever I heard one. The City shark was different. If a chap must go a-robbing, that sort of fellow is fair game. But your friend, and then the girls — well, I say again, I couldn't have believed it."

"Then why believe it?"

"Because it *is* so."

"Well, you seem to have persuaded yourself to that effect. You don't seem to have much evidence to lay before any one else."

"I could swear to you in a police-court. What put the lid on it was that when you were cutting my wire — and an infernal liberty it was! — I saw that white tuft of yours sticking out from behind your mask."

For the first time an acute observer might have seen some slight sign of emotion upon the face of the baronet.

"You seem to have a fairly vivid imagination," said he.

His visitor flushed with anger.

"See here, Hailworthy," said he, opening his hand and showing a small, jagged triangle of black cloth. "Do you see that? It was on the ground near the car of the young women. You must have ripped it off as you jumped out from your seat. Now send for that heavy black driving-coat of yours. If you don't ring the bell I'll ring it myself, and we shall have it in. I'm going to see this thing through, and don't you make any mistake about that."

The baronet's answer was a surprising one. He rose, passed Barker's chair, and, walking over to the door, he locked it and placed the key in his pocket.

"You *are* going to see it through," said he. "I'll lock you in until you do. Now we must have a straight talk, Barker, as man to man, and whether it ends in tragedy or not depends on you."

He had half-opened one of the drawers in his desk as he spoke. His visitor frowned in anger.

"You won't make matters any better by threatening me, Hailworthy. I am going to do my duty, and you won't bluff me out of it."

"I have no wish to bluff you. When I spoke of a tragedy I did not mean to you. What I meant was that there are some turns which this affair cannot be allowed to take. I have neither kith nor kin, but there is the family honour, and some things are impossible."

"It is late to talk like that."

"Well, perhaps it is; but not too late. And now I have a good deal to say to you. First of all, you are quite right, and it was I who held you up last night on the Mayfield road."

"But why on earth — "

"All right. Let me tell it my own way. First I want you to look at these." He unlocked a drawer and he took out two small packages. "These were to be posted in London to-night. This one is addressed to you, and I may as well hand it over to you at once. It contains your watch and your purse. So, you see, bar your cut wire you would have been none the worse for your adventure. This other packet is addressed to the young ladies of the Gaiety Theatre, and their properties are enclosed. I hope I have convinced you that I had intended full reparation in each case before you came to accuse me?"

"Well?" asked Barker.

"Well, we will now deal with Sir George Wilde, who is, as you may not know, the senior partner of Wilde and Guggendorf, the founders of the Ludgate

Bank of infamous memory. His chauffeur is a case apart. You may take it from me, upon my word of honour, that I had plans for the chauffeur. But it is the master that I want to speak of. You know that I am not a rich man myself. I expect all the county knows that. When Black Tulip lost the Derby I was hard hit. And other things as well. Then I had a legacy of a thousand. This infernal bank was paying 7 per cent. on deposits. I knew Wilde. I saw him. I asked him if it was safe. He said it was. I paid it in, and within forty-eight hours the whole thing went to bits. It came out before the Official Receiver that Wilde had known for three months that nothing could save him. And yet he took all my cargo aboard his sinking vessel. He was all right — confound him! He had plenty besides. But I had lost all my money and no law could help me. Yet he had robbed me as clearly as one man could rob another. I saw him and he laughed in my face. Told me to stick to Consols, and that the lesson was cheap at the price. So I just swore that, by hook or by crook, I would get level with him. I knew his habits, for I had made it my business to do so. I knew that he came back from Eastbourne on Sunday nights. I knew that he carried a good sum with him in his pocket-book. Well it's *my* pocket-book now. Do you mean to tell me that I'm not morally justified in what I have done? By the Lord, I'd have left the devil as bare as he left many a widow and orphan, if I'd had the time!"

"That's all very well. But what about me? What about the girls?"

"Have some common sense, Barker. Do you suppose that I could go and stick up this one personal enemy of mine and escape detection? It was impossible. I was bound to make myself out to be just a common robber who had run up against him by accident. So I turned myself loose on the high road and took my chance. As the devil would have it, the first man I met was yourself. I was a fool not to recognise that old ironmonger's store of yours by the row it made coming up the hill. When I saw you I could hardly speak for laughing. But I was bound to carry it through. The same with the actresses. I'm afraid I gave myself away, for I couldn't take their little fal-lals, but I had to keep up a show. Then came my man himself. There was no bluff about that. I was out to skin him, and I did. Now, Barker, what do you think of it all? I had a pistol at your head last night, and, by George! whether you believe it or not, you have one at mine this morning!"

The young man rose slowly, and with a broad smile he wrung the magistrate by the hand.

"Don't do it again. It's too risky," said he. "The swine would score heavily if you were taken."

"You're a good chap, Barker," said the magistrate. "No, I won't do it again. Who's the fellow who talks of 'one crowded hour of glorious life'? By George! it's too fascinating. I had the time of my life! Talk of fox-hunting! No, I'll never touch it again, for it might get a grip of me."

A telephone rang sharply upon the table, and the baronet put the receiver to his ear. As he listened he smiled across at his companion.

"I'm rather late this morning," said he, "and

they are waiting for me to try some petty larcenies
on the county bench."

III. A POINT OF VIEW

It was an American journalist who was writing up England — or writing her down as the mood seized him. Sometimes he blamed and sometimes he praised, and the case-hardened old country actually went its way all the time quite oblivious of his approval or of his disfavour — being ready at all times, through some queer mental twist, to say more bitter things and more unjust ones about herself than any critic could ever venture upon. However, in the course of his many columns in the *New York Clarion* our journalist did at last get through somebody's skin in the way that is here narrated.

It was a kindly enough article upon English country-house life in which he had described a visit paid for a week-end to Sir Henry Trustall's. There was only a single critical passage in it, and it was one which he had written with a sense both of journalistic and of democratic satisfaction. In it he had sketched off the lofty obsequiousness of the flunkey who had ministered to his needs. "He seemed to take a smug satisfaction in his own degradation," said he. "Surely the last spark of manhood must have gone from the man who has so entirely lost his own individuality. He revelled in humility. He was an instrument of service — nothing more."

Some months had passed and our American Pressman had recorded impressions from St. Petersburg to Madrid. He was on his homeward way when once again he found himself the guest of Sir Henry. He had returned from an afternoon's shooting, and had finished dressing when there was a knock at the door and the footman entered. He was a large cleanly-built man, as is proper to a class who are chosen with a keener eye to physique than any crack regiment. The American supposed that the man had entered to perform some menial service, but to his surprise he softly closed the door behind him.

"Might I have a word with you, sir, if you can kindly give me a moment?" he said in the velvety voice which always got upon the visitor's republican nerves.

"Well, what is it?" the journalist asked sharply.

"It's this, sir." The footman drew from his breast-pocket the copy of the *Clarion*. "A friend over the water chanced to see this, sir, and he thought it would be of interest to me. So he sent it."

"Well?"

"You wrote it, sir, I fancy."

"What if I did."

"And this 'ere footman is your idea of me."

The American glanced at the passage and approved his own phrases.

"Yes, that's you," he admitted.

The footman folded up his document once more and replaced it in his pocket.

"I'd like to 'ave a word or two with you over that, sir," he said in the same suave imperturbable voice. "I don't think, sir, that you quite see the thing from our point of view. I'd like to put it to you as I see it myself. Maybe it would strike you different then."

The American became interested. There was "copy" in the air.

"Sit down," said he.

"No, sir, begging your pardon, sir, I'd very much rather stand."

"Well, do as you please. If you've got anything to say, get ahead with it."

"You see, sir, it's like this: There's a tradition — what you might call a standard — among the best servants, and it's 'anded down from one to the other. When I joined I was a third, and my chief and the butler were both old men who had been trained by the best. I took after them just as they took after those that went before them. It goes back away further than you can tell."

"I can understand that."

"But what perhaps you don't so well understand, sir, is the spirit that's lying behind it. There's a man's own private self-respect to which you allude, sir, in this 'ere article. That's his own. But he can't keep it, so far as I can see, unless he returns good service for the good money that he takes."

"Well, he can do that without — without — crawling."

The footman's florid face paled a little at the word. Apparently he was not quite the automatic machine that he appeared.

"By your leave, sir, we'll come to that later," said he. "But I want you to understand what we are trying to do even when you don't approve of our way of doing it. We are trying to make life smooth and easy for our master and for our master's guests. We do it in the way that's been 'anded down to us as the best way. If our master could suggest any better way, then it would be our place either to leave his service if we disapproved it, or else to try and do it as he wanted. It would hurt the self-respect of any good servant to take a man's money and not give him the very best he can in return for it."

"Well," said the American, "it's not quite as we see it in America."

"That's right, sir. I was over there last year with Sir Henry — in New York, sir, and I saw something of the men-servants and their ways. They were paid for service, sir, and they did not give what they were paid for. You talk about self-respect, sir, in this article. Well now, my self-respect wouldn't let me treat a master as I've seen them do over there."

"We don't even like the word 'master,'" said the American.

"Well, that's neither 'ere nor there, sir, if I may be so bold as to say so. If you're serving a gentleman he's your master for the time being and any name you may choose to call it by don't make no difference. But you can't eat your cake and 'ave it, sir. You can't sell your independence and 'ave it, too."

"Maybe not," said the American. "All the same, the fact remains that your manhood is the worse for it."

"There I don't 'old with you, sir."

"If it were not, you wouldn't be standing there arguing so quietly. You'd speak to me in another tone, I guess."

"You must remember, sir, that you are my master's guest, and that I am paid to wait upon you and make your visit a pleasant one. So long as you are 'ere, sir, that is 'ow I regard it. Now in London — "

"Well, what about London?"

"Well, in London if you would have the goodness to let me have a word with you I could make you understand a little clearer what I am trying to explain to you. 'Arding is my name, sir. If you get a call from 'Enery 'Arding, you'll know that I 'ave a word to say to you."

* * * * *

So it happened about three days later that our American journalist in his London hotel received a letter that a Mr. Henry Harding desired to speak with him. The man was waiting in the hall dressed in quiet tweeds. He had cast his manner with his uniform and was firmly deliberate in all he said and did. The professional silkiness was gone, and his bearing was all that the most democratic could desire.

"It's courteous of you to see me, sir," said he. "There's that matter of the article still open between us, and I would like to have a word or two more about it."

"Well, I can give you just ten minutes," said the American journalist.

"I understand that you are a busy man, sir, so I'll cut it as short as I can. There's a public garden opposite if you would be so good as talk it over in the open air."

The Pressman took his hat and accompanied the footman. They walked together down the winding gravelled path among the rhododendron bushes.

"It's like this, sir," said the footman, halting when they had arrived at a quiet nook. "I was hoping that you would see it in our light and understand me when I told you that the servant who was trying to give honest service for his master's money, and the man who is free born and as good as his neighbour are two separate folk. There's the duty man and there's the natural man, and they are different men. To say that I have no life of my own, or self-respect of my own, because there are days when I give myself to the service of another, is not fair treatment. I was hoping, sir, that when I made this clear to you, you would have met me like a man and taken it back."

"Well, you have not convinced me," said the American. "A man's a man, and he's responsible for all his actions."

"Then you won't take back what you said of me — the degradation and the rest?"

"No, I don't see why I should."

The man's comely face darkened.

"You *will* take it back," said he. "I'll smash your blasted head if you don't."

The American was suddenly aware that he was in the presence of a very ugly proposition. The man was large, strong, and evidently most earnest and determined. His brows were knotted, his eyes flashing, and his fists clenched. On neutral ground he struck the journalist as really being a very different person to the obsequious and silken footman of Trustall Old Manor. The American had all the courage, both of his race and of his profession, but he realised suddenly that he was very much in the wrong. He was man enough to say so.

"Well, sir, this once," said the footman, as they shook hands. "I don't approve of the mixin' of classes — none of the best servants do. But I'm on my own to-day, so we'll let it pass. But I wish you'd set it right with your people, sir. I wish you would make them understand that an English servant can give good and proper service and yet that he's a human bein' I after all."

IV. THE FALL OF LORD BARRYMORE

These are few social historians of those days who have not told of the long and fierce struggle between those two famous bucks, Sir Charles Tregellis and Lord Barrymore, for the Lordship of the Kingdom of St. James, a struggle which divided the whole of fashionable London into two opposing camps. It has been chronicled also how the peer retired suddenly and the commoner resumed his great career without a rival. Only here, however, one can read the real and remarkable reason for this sudden eclipse of a star.

It was one morning in the days of this famous struggle that Sir Charles Tregellis was performing his very complicated toilet, and Ambrose, his valet, was helping him to attain that pitch of perfection which had long gained him the reputation of being the best-dressed man in town. Suddenly Sir Charles paused, his *coup d'archet* half-executed, the final beauty of his neck-cloth half-achieved, while he listened with surprise and indignation upon his large, comely, fresh-complexioned face. Below, the decorous hum of Jermyn Street had been broken by the sharp, staccato, metallic beating of a doorknocker.

"I begin to think that this uproar must be at our door," said Sir Charles, as one who thinks aloud. "For five minutes it has come and gone; yet Perkins has his orders."

At a gesture from his master Ambrose stepped out upon the balcony and craned his discreet head over it. From the street below came a voice, drawling but clear.

"You would oblige me vastly, fellow, if you would do me the favour to open this door," said the voice.

"Who is it? What is it?" asked the scandalised Sir Charles, with his arrested elbow still pointing upwards.

Ambrose had returned with as much surprise upon his dark face as the etiquette of his position would allow him to show.

"It is a young gentleman, Sir Charles."

"A young gentleman? There is no one in London who is not aware that I do not show before midday. Do you know the person? Have you seen him before?"

"I have not seen him, sir, but he is very like some one I could name."

"Like some one? Like whom?"

"With all respect, Sir Charles, I could for a moment have believed that it was yourself when I looked down. A smaller man, sir, and a youth; but the voice, the face, the bearing — "

"It must be that young cub Vereker, my brother's ne'er-do-weel," muttered Sir Charles, continuing his toilet. "I have heard that there are points in which he resembles me. He wrote from Oxford that he would come, and I answered that I would not see him. Yet he ventures to insist. The fellow needs a lesson! Ambrose, ring for Perkins."

A large footman entered with an outraged expression upon his face.

"I cannot have this uproar at the door, Perkins!"

"If you please, the young gentleman won't go away, sir."

"Won't go away? It is your duty to see that he goes away. Have you not your orders? Didn't you tell him that I am not seen before midday?"

"I said so, sir. He would have pushed his way in, for all I could say, so I slammed the door in his face."

"Very right, Perkins."

"But now, sir, he is making such a din that all the folk are at the windows. There is a crowd gathering in the street, sir."

From below came the crack-crack-crack of the knocker, ever rising in insistence, with a chorus of laughter and encouraging comments from the spectators. Sir Charles flushed with anger. There must be some limit to such impertinence.

"My clouded amber cane is in the corner," said he. "Take it with you, Perkins. I give you a free hand. A stripe or two may bring the young rascal to reason."

The large Perkins smiled and departed. The door was heard to open below and the knocker was at rest. A few moments later there followed a prolonged howl and a noise as of a beaten carpet. Sir Charles listened with a smile which gradually faded from his good-humoured face.

"The fellow must not overdo it," he muttered. "I would not do the lad an injury, whatever his deserts may be. Ambrose, run out on the balcony and call him off. This has gone far enough."

But before the valet could move there came the swift patter of agile feet upon the stairs, and a handsome youth, dressed in the height of fashion, was standing framed in the open doorway. The pose, the face, above all the curious, mischievous, dancing light in the large blue eyes, all spoke of the famous Tregellis blood. Even such was Sir Charles when, twenty years before, he had, by virtue of his spirit and audacity, in one short season taken a place in London from which Brummell himself had afterwards vainly struggled to depose him. The youth faced the angry features of his uncle with an air of debonair amusement, and he held towards him, upon his outstretched palms, the broken fragments of an amber cane.

"I much fear, sir," said he, "that in correcting your fellow I have had the misfortune to injure what can only have been your property. I am vastly concerned that it should have occurred."

Sir Charles stared with intolerant eyes at this impertinent apparition. The other looked back in a laughable parody of his senior's manner. As Ambrose had remarked after his inspection from the balcony, the two were very alike, save that the younger was smaller, finer cut, and the more nervously alive of the two.

"You arc my nephew, Vereker Tregellis?" asked Sir Charles.

"Yours to command, sir."

"I hear bad reports of you from Oxford."

"Yes, sir, I understand that the reports *are* bad."

"Nothing could be worse."

"So I have been told."

"Why are you here, sir?"

"That I might see my famous uncle."

"So you made a tumult in his street, forced his door, and beat his footman?"

"Yes, sir."

"You had my letter?"

"Yes, sir."

"You were told that I was not receiving?"

"Yes, sir."

"I can remember no such exhibition of impertinence."

The young man smiled and rubbed his hands in satisfaction.

"There is an impertinence which is redeemed by wit," said Sir Charles, severely. "There is another which is the mere boorishness of the clodhopper. As you grow older and wiser you may discern the difference."

"You are very right, sir," said the young man,

warmly. "The finer shades of impertinence are infinitely subtle, and only experience and the society of one who is a recognised master" — here he bowed to his uncle — "can enable one to excel."

Sir Charles was notoriously touchy in temper for the first hour after his morning chocolate. He allowed himself to show it.

"I cannot congratulate my brother upon his son," said he. "I had hoped for something more worthy of our traditions."

"Perhaps, sir, upon a longer acquaintance — "

"The chance is too small to justify the very irksome experience. I must ask you, sir, to bring to a close a visit which never should have been made."

The young man smiled affably, but gave no sign of departure.

"May I ask, sir," said he, in an easy conversational fashion, "whether you can recall Principal Munro, of my college?"

"No, sir, I cannot," his uncle answered, sharply.

"Naturally you would not burden your memory to such an extent, but he still remembers you. In some conversation with him yesterday he did me the honour to say that I brought you back to his recollection by what he was pleased to call the mingled levity and obstinacy of my character. The levity seems to have already impressed you. I am now reduced to showing you the obstinacy." He sat down in a chair near the door and folded his arms, still beaming pleasantly at his uncle.

"Oh, you won't go?" asked Sir Charles, grimly.

"No, sir; I will stay."

"Ambrose, step down and call a couple of chairmen."

"I should not advise it, sir. They will be hurt."

"I will put you out with my own hands."

"That, sir, you can always do. As my uncle, I could scarce resist you. But, short of throwing me down the stair, I do not see how you can avoid giving me half an hour of your attention."

Sir Charles smiled. He could not help it. There was so much that was reminiscent of his own arrogant and eventful youth in the bearing of this youngster. He was mollified, too, by the defiance of menials and quick submission to himself. He turned to the glass and signed to Ambrose to continue his duties.

"I must ask you to await the conclusion of my toilet," said he. "Then we shall see how far you can justify such an intrusion."

When the valet had at last left the room Sir Charles turned his attention once more to his scapegrace nephew, who had viewed the details of the famous buck's toilet with the face of an acolyte assisting at a mystery.

"Now, sir," said the older man, "speak, and speak to the point, for I can assure you that I have many more important matters which claim my attention. The Prince is waiting for me at the present instant at Carlton House. Be as brief as you can. What is it that you want?"

"A thousand pounds."

"Really! Nothing more?" Sir Charles had turned acid again.

"Yes, sir; an introduction to Mr. Brinsley Sheridan, whom I know to be your friend."

"And why to him?"

"Because I am told that he controls Drury Lane Theatre, and I have a fancy to be an actor. My friends assure me that I have a pretty talent that way."

"I can see you clearly, sir, in Charles Surface, or any other part where a foppish insolence is the essential. The less you acted, the better you would be. But it is absurd to suppose that I could help you to such a career. I could not justify it to your father. Return to Oxford at once, and continue your studies."

"Impossible!"

"And pray, sir, what is the impediment?"

"I think I may have mentioned to you that I had an interview yesterday with the Principal. He ended it by remarking that the authorities of the University could tolerate me no more."

"Sent down?"

"Yes, sir."

"And this is the fruit, no doubt, of a long series of rascalities."

"Something of the sort, sir, I admit."

In spite of himself, Sir Charles began once more to relax in his severity towards this handsome young scapegrace. His absolute frankness disarmed criticism. It was in a more gracious voice that the older man continued the conversation.

"Why do you want this large sum of money?" he asked.

"To pay my college debts before I go, sir."

"Your father is not a rich man."

"No, sir. I could not apply to him for that reason."

"So you come to me, who am a stranger!"

"No, sir, no! You are my uncle, and, if I may say so, my ideal and my model."

"You flatter me, my good Vereker. But if you think you can flatter me out of a thousand pounds, you mistake your man. I will give you no money."

"Of course, sir, if you can't — "

"I did not say I can't. I say I won't."

"If you can, sir, I think you will."

Sir Charles smiled, and flicked his sleeve with his lace handkerchief.

"I find you vastly entertaining," said he. "Pray continue your conversation. Why do you think that I will give you so large a sum of money?"

"The reason that I think so," continued the

younger man, "is that I can do you a service which will seem to you worth a thousand pounds."

Sir Charles raised his eyebrows in surprise.

"Is this blackmail?" he inquired.

Vereker Tregellis flushed.

"Sir," said he, with a pleasing sternness, "you surprise me. You should know the blood of which I come too well to suppose that I would attempt such a thing."

"I am relieved to hear that there are limits to what you consider to be justifiable. I must confess that I had seen none in your conduct up to now. But you say that you can do me a service which will be worth a thousand pounds to me?"

"Yes, sir."

"And pray, sir, what may this service be?"

"To make Lord Barrymore the laughing-stock of the town."

Sir Charles, in spite of himself, lost for an instant the absolute serenity of his self-control. He started, and his face expressed his surprise. By what devilish instinct did this raw undergraduate find the one chink in his armour? Deep in his heart, unacknowledged to any one, there was the will to pay many a thousand pounds to the man who would bring ridicule upon this his most dangerous rival, who was challenging his supremacy in fashionable London.

"Did you come from Oxford with this precious

project?" he asked, after a pause.

"No, sir. I chanced to see the man himself last night, and I conceived an ill-will to him, and would do him a mischief."

"Where did you see him?"

"I spent the evening, sir, at the Vauxhall Gardens."

"No doubt you would," interpolated his uncle.

"My Lord Barrymore was there. He was attended by one who was dressed as a clergyman, but who was, as I am told, none other than Hooper the Tinman, who acts as his bully and thrashes all who may offend him. Together they passed down the central path, insulting the women and browbeating the men. They actually hustled me. I was offended, sir — so much so that I nearly took the matter in hand then and there."

"It is as well that you did not. The prizefighter would have beaten you."

"Perhaps so, sir — and also, perhaps not."

"Ah, you add pugilism to your elegant accomplishments?"

The young man laughed pleasantly.

"William Ball is the only professor of my Alma Mater who has ever had occasion to compliment me, sir. He is better known as the Oxford Pet. I think, with all modesty, that I could hold him for a dozen rounds. But last night I suffered the annoyance without protest, for since it is said that the same scene is enacted every evening, there is always time to act."

"And how would you act, may I ask?"

"That, sir, I should prefer to keep to myself; but my aim, as I say, would be to make Lord Barrymore a laughing-stock to all London."

Sir Charles cogitated for a moment.

"Pray, sir," said he, "why did you imagine that any humiliation to Lord Barrymore would be pleasing to me?"

"Even in the provinces we know something of what passes in polite circles. Your antagonism to this man is to be found in every column of fashionable gossip. The town is divided between you. It is impossible that any public slight upon him should be unpleasing to you."

Sir Charles smiled.

"You are a shrewd reasoner," said he. "We will suppose for the instant that you are right. Can you give me no hint what means you would adopt to attain this very desirable end?"

"I would merely make the remark, sir, that many women have been wronged by this fellow. That is a matter of common knowledge. If one of these damsels were to upbraid him in public in such a fashion that the sympathy of the bystanders should be with her, then I can imagine, if she were sufficiently persistent, that his lordship's position might become an unenviable one."

"And you know such a woman?"

"I think, sir, that I do."

"Well, my good Vereker, if any such attempt is in your mind, I see no reason why I should stand between Lord Barrymore and the angry fair. As to whether the result is worth a thousand pounds, I can make no promise."

"You shall yourself be the judge, sir."

"I will be an exacting judge, nephew."

"Very good, sir; I should not desire otherwise. If things go as I hope, his lordship will not show face in St. James's Street for a year to come. I will now, if I may, give you your instructions."

"My instructions! What do you mean? I have nothing to do with the matter."

"You are the judge, sir, and therefore must be present."

"I can play no part."

"No, sir. I would not ask you to do more than be a witness."

"What, then, are my instructions, as you are pleased to call them?"

"You will come to the Gardens to-night, uncle, at nine o'clock precisely. You will walk down the centre path, and you will seat yourself upon one of the rustic seats which are beside the statue of Aphrodite. You will wait and you will observe."

"Very good; I will do so. I begin to perceive, nephew, that the breed of Tregellis has not yet lost some of the points which have made it famous."

It was at the stroke of nine that night when Sir Charles, throwing his reins to the groom, descended from his high yellow phaeton, which forthwith turned to take its place in the long line of fashionable carriages waiting for their owners. As he entered the gate of the Gardens, the centre at that time of the dissipation and revelry of London, he turned up the collar of his driving-cape and drew his hat over his eyes, for he had no desire to be personally associated with what might well prove to be a public scandal. In spite of his attempted disguise, however, there was that in his walk and his carriage which caused many an eye to be turned after him as he passed and many a hand to be raised in salute. Sir Charles walked on, and, seating himself upon the rustic bench in front of the famous statue, which was in the very middle of the Gardens, he waited in amused suspense to see the next act in this comedy.

From the pavilion, whence the paths radiated, there came the strains of the band of the Foot Guards, and by the many-coloured lamps twinkling from every tree Sir Charles could see the confused whirl of the dancers. Suddenly the music stopped. The quadrilles were at an end.

An instant afterwards the central path by which he sat was thronged by the revellers. In a many-coloured crowd, stocked and cravated with all the bravery of buff and plum-colour and blue, the bucks of the town passed and repassed with their high-waisted, straight-skirted, be-bonneted ladies upon their arms.

It was not a decorous assembly. Many of the men, flushed and noisy, had come straight from their potations. The women, too, were loud and aggressive. Now and then, with a rush and a swirl, amid a chorus of screams from the girls and good-humoured laughter from their escorts, some band of high-blooded, noisy youths would break their way across the moving throng. It was no place for the prim or demure, and there was a spirit of good-nature and merriment among the crowd which condoned the wildest liberty.

And yet there were some limits to what could be tolerated even by so Bohemian an assembly. A murmur of anger followed in the wake of two roisterers who were making their way down the path. It would, perhaps, be fairer to say one roisterer; for of the two it was only the first who carried himself with such insolence, although it was the second who ensured that he could do it with impunity.

The leader was a very tall, hatchet-faced man, dressed in the very height of fashion, whose evil, handsome features were flushed with wine and arrogance. He shouldered his way roughly through the crowd, peering with an abominable smile into the faces of the women, and occasionally, where the weakness of the escort invited an insult, stretching out his hand and caressing the cheek or neck of some passing girl, laughing loudly as she winced away from his touch.

Close at his heels walked his hired attendant, whom, out of insolent caprice and with a desire to show his contempt for the prejudices of others, he had dressed as a rough country clergyman. This fellow slouched along with frowning brows and surly, challenging eyes, like some faithful, hideous human bulldog, his knotted hands protruding from his rusty cassock, his great underhung jaw turning slowly from right to left as he menaced the crowd with his sinister gaze. Already a close observer might have marked upon his face a heaviness and looseness of feature, the first signs of that physical decay which in a very few years was to stretch him, a helpless wreck, too weak to utter his own name, upon the causeway of the London streets. At present, however, he was still an unbeaten man, the terror of the Ring, and as his ill-omened face was seen behind his infamous master many a half-raised cane was lowered and many a hot word was checked, while the whisper of "Hooper! 'Ware Bully Hooper!" warned all who were aggrieved that it might be best to pocket their injuries lest some even worse thing should befall them. Many a maimed and disfigured man had carried away from Vauxhall the handiwork of the Tinman and his patron.

Moving in insolent slowness through the crowd, the bully and his master had just come opposite to the bench upon which sat Sir Charles Tregellis. At this place the path opened up into a circular space, brilliantly illuminated and surrounded by rustic seats. From one of these an elderly, ringleted woman, deeply veiled, rose suddenly and barred the path of the swaggering nobleman. Her voice sounded clear and strident above the babel of tongues, which hushed suddenly that their owners might hear it.

"Marry her, my lord! I entreat you to marry her! Oh, surely you will marry my poor Amelia!" said the voice.

Lord Barrymore stood aghast. From all sides folk were closing in and heads were peering over shoulders. He tried to push on, but the lady barred his way and two palms pressed upon his beruffled front.

"Surely, surely you would not desert her! Take the advice of that good, kind clergyman behind you!" wailed the voice. "Oh, be a man of honour and marry her!"

The elderly lady thrust out her hand and drew forward a lumpish-looking young woman, who sobbed and mopped her eyes with her handkerchief.

"The plague take you!" roared his lordship, in a fury. "Who is the wench? I vow that I never clapped eyes on either of you in my life!"

"It is my niece Amelia," cried the lady, "your own loving Amelia! Oh, my lord, can you pretend that you have forgotten poor, trusting Amelia, of Woodbine Cottage at Lichfield."

"I never set foot in Lichfield in my life!" cried the peer. "You are two impostors who should be whipped at the cart's tail."

"Oh, wicked! Oh, Amelia!" screamed the lady, in a voice that resounded through the Gardens. "Oh, my darling, try to soften his hard heart; pray him that he make an honest woman of you at last."

With a lurch the stout young woman fell forward and embraced Lord Barrymore with the hug of a bear. He would have raised his cane, but his arms were pinned to his sides.

"Hooper! Hooper!" screamed the furious peer, craning his neck in horror, for the girl seemed to be trying to kiss him.

But the bruiser, as he ran forward, found himself entangled with the old lady.

"Out o' the way, marm!" he cried. "Out o' the way, I say!" and pushed her violently aside.

"Oh, you rude, rude man!" she shrieked, springing back in front of him. "He hustled me, good people; you saw him hustle me! A clergyman, but no gentleman! What! you would treat a lady so — you would do it again? Oh, I could slap, slap, slap you!"

And with each repetition of the word, with extraordinary swiftness, her open palm rang upon the prizefighter's cheek.

The crowd buzzed with amazement and delight.

"Hooper! Hooper!" cried Lord Barrymore once more, for he was still struggling in the ever-closer embrace of the unwieldy and amorous Amelia.

The bully again pushed forward to the aid of his patron, but again the elderly lady confronted him, her head back, her left arm extended, her whole attitude, to his amazement, that of an expert boxer.

The prizefighter's brutal nature was roused. Woman or no woman, he would show the murmuring crowd what it meant to cross the path of the Tinman. She had struck him. She must take the consequence. No one should square up to him with impunity. He swung his right with a curse. The bonnet instantly ducked under his arm, and a line of razor-like knuckles left an open cut under his eye.

Amid wild cries of delight and encouragement from the dense circle of spectators, the lady danced round the sham clergyman, dodging his ponderous blows, slipping under his arms, and smacking back at him most successfully. Once she tripped and fell over her own skirt, but was up and at him again in an instant.

"You vulgar fellow!" she shrieked. "Would you strike a helpless woman! Take that! Oh, you rude and ill-bred man!"

Bully Hooper was cowed for the first time in his life by the extraordinary thing that he was fighting. The creature was as elusive as a shadow, and yet the blood was dripping down his chin from the effects of the blows. He shrank back with an amazed face from so uncanny an antagonist. And in the moment that he did so his spell was for ever broken. Only success could hold it. A check was fatal. In all the crowd there was scarce one who was not nursing some grievance against master or man, and waiting for that moment of weakness in which to revenge it.

With a growl of rage the circle closed in. There was an eddy of furious, struggling men, with Lord Barrymore's thin, flushed face and Hooper's bulldog jowl in the centre of it. A moment after they were both upon the ground, and a dozen sticks were rising and falling above them.

"Let me up! You're killing me! For God's sake let me up!" cried a crackling voice.

Hooper fought mute, like the bulldog he was, till his senses were beaten out of him.

Bruised, kicked, and mauled, never did their worst victim come so badly from the Gardens as the bully and his patron that night. But worse than the ache of wounds for Lord Barrymore was the smart of the mind as he thought how every club and drawing-room in London would laugh for a week to come at the tale of his Amelia and her aunt.

Sir Charles had stood, rocking with laughter, upon the bench which overlooked the scene. When at last he made his way back through the crowds to his yellow phaeton, he was not entirely surprised to find that the back seat was already occupied by two giggling females, who were exchanging most unladylike repartees with the attendant grooms.

"You young rascals!" he remarked, over his shoulder, as he gathered up his reins.

The two females tittered loudly.

"Uncle Charles!" cried the elder, "may I present Mr. Jack Jarvis, of Brasenose College? I think, uncle, you should take us somewhere to sup, for it has been a vastly fatiguing performance. To-morrow I will do myself the honour to call, at your convenience, and will venture to bring with me the receipt for one thousand pounds."

V. THE HORROR OF THE HEIGHTS (WHICH INCLUDES THE MANUSCRIPT KNOWN AS THE JOYCE-ARMSTRONG FRAGMENT)

The idea that the extraordinary narrative which has been called the Joyce-Armstrong Fragment is an elaborate practical joke evolved by some unknown person, cursed by a perverted and sinister sense of humour, has now been abandoned by all who have examined the matter. The most *macabre* and imaginative of plotters would hesitate before linking his morbid fancies with the unquestioned and tragic facts which reinforce the statement. Though the assertions contained in it are amazing and even monstrous, it is none the less forcing itself upon the general intelligence that they are true, and that we must readjust our ideas to the new situation. This world of ours appears to be separated by a slight and precarious margin of safety from a most singular and unexpected danger. I will endeavour in this narrative, which reproduces the original document in its necessarily somewhat fragmentary form, to lay before the reader the whole of the facts up to date, prefacing my statement by saying that, if there be any who doubt the narrative of Joyce-Armstrong, there can be no question at all as to the facts concerning Lieutenant Myrtle, R.N., and Mr. Hay Connor, who undoubtedly met their end in the manner described.

The Joyce-Armstrong Fragment was found in the field which is called Lower Haycock, lying one mile to the westward of the village of Withyham, upon the Kent and Sussex border. It was on the fifteenth of September last that an agricultural labourer, James Flynn, in the employment of Mathew Dodd, farmer, of the Chauntry Farm, Withyham, perceived a briar pipe lying near the footpath which skirts the hedge in Lower Haycock. A few paces farther on he picked up a pair of broken binocular glasses. Finally, among some nettles in the ditch, he caught sight of a flat, canvas-backed book, which proved to be a note-book with detachable leaves, some of which had come loose and were fluttering along the base of the hedge. These he collected, but some, including the first, were never recovered, and leave a deplorable hiatus in this all-important statement. The notebook was taken by the labourer to his master, who in turn showed it to Dr. J. H. Atherton, of Hartfield. This gentleman at once recognised the need for an expert examination, and the manuscript was forwarded to the Aero Club in London, where it now lies.

The first two pages of the manuscript are missing. There is also one torn away at the end of the narrative, though none of these affect the general coherence of the story. It is conjectured that the missing opening is concerned with the record of Mr. Joyce-Armstrong's qualifications as an aeronaut, which can be gathered from other sources and are admitted to be unsurpassed among the air-pilots of England. For many years he has been looked upon as among the most daring and the most intellectual of flying men, a combination which has enabled him to both invent and test several new devices, including the common gyroscopic attachment which is known by his name. The main body of the manuscript is written neatly in ink, but the last few lines are in pencil and are so ragged as to be hardly legible — exactly, in fact, as they might be expected to appear if they were scribbled off hurriedly from the seat of a moving aeroplane. There are, it may be added, several stains, both on the last page and on the outside cover, which have been pronounced by the Home Office experts to be blood — probably human and certainly mammalian. The fact that something closely resembling the organism of malaria was discovered in this blood, and that Joyce-Armstrong is known to have suffered from intermittent fever, is a remarkable example of the new weapons which modern science has placed in the hands of our detectives.

And now a word as to the personality of the author of this epoch-making statement. Joyce-Armstrong, according to the few friends who really knew something of the man, was a poet and a dreamer, as well as a mechanic and an inventor. He was a man of considerable wealth, much of which he had spent in the pursuit of his aeronautical hobby. He had four private aeroplanes in his hangars near Devizes, and is said to have made no fewer than one hundred and seventy ascents in the course of last year. He was a retiring man with dark moods, in which he would avoid the society of his fellows. Captain Dangerfield, who knew him better than any one, says that there were times when his eccentricity threatened to develop into something more serious. His habit of carrying a shot-gun with him in his aeroplane was one manifestation of it.

Another was the morbid effect which the fall of

Lieutenant Myrtle had upon his mind. Myrtle, who was attempting the height record, fell from an altitude of something over thirty thousand feet. Horrible to narrate, his head was entirely obliterated, though his body and limbs preserved their configuration. At every gathering of airmen, Joyce-Armstrong, according to Dangerfield, would ask, with an enigmatic smile: "And where, pray, is Myrtle's head?"

On another occasion after dinner, at the mess of the Flying School on Salisbury Plain, he started a debate as to what will be the most permanent danger which airmen will have to encounter. Having listened to successive opinions as to air-pockets, faulty construction, and over-banking, he ended by shrugging his shoulders and refusing to put forward his own views, though he gave the impression that they differed from any advanced by his companions.

It is worth remarking that after his own complete disappearance it was found that his private affairs were arranged with a precision which may show that he had a strong premonition of disaster. With these essential explanations I will now give the narrative exactly as it stands, beginning at page three of the blood-soaked note-book: —

"Nevertheless, when I dined at Rheims with Coselli and Gustav Raymond I found that neither of them was aware of any particular danger in the higher layers of the atmosphere. I did not actually say what was in my thoughts, but I got so near to it that if they had any corresponding idea they could not have failed to express it. But then they are two empty, vainglorious fellows with no thought beyond seeing their silly names in the newspaper. It is interesting to note that neither of them had ever been much beyond the twenty-thousand-foot level. Of course, men have been higher than this both in balloons and in the ascent of mountains. It must be well above that point that the aeroplane enters the danger zone — always presuming that my premonitions are correct.

"Aeroplaning has been with us now for more than twenty years, and one might well ask: Why should this peril be only revealing itself in our day? The answer is obvious. In the old days of weak engines, when a hundred horse-power Gnome or Green was considered ample for every need, the flights were very restricted. Now that three hundred horse-power is the rule rather than the exception, visits to the upper layers have become easier and more common. Some of us can remember how, in our youth, Garros made a world-wide reputation by attaining nineteen thousand feet, and it was considered a remarkable achievement to fly over the Alps. Our standard now has been immeasurably raised, and there are twenty high flights for one in former years. Many of them have been undertaken with impunity. The thirty-thousand-foot level has been reached time after time with no discomfort beyond cold and asthma. What does this prove? A visitor might descend upon this planet a thousand times and never see a tiger. Yet tigers exist, and if he chanced to come down into a jungle he might be devoured. There are jungles of the upper air, and there are worse things than tigers which inhabit them. I believe in time they will map these jungles accurately out. Even at the present moment I could name two of them. One of them lies over the Pau-Biarritz district of France. Another is just over my head as I write here in my house in Wiltshire. I rather think there is a third in the Homburg-Wies-baden district.

"It was the disappearance of the airmen that first set me thinking. Of course, every one said that they had fallen into the sea, but that did not satisfy me at all. First, there was Verrier in France; his machine was found near Bayonne, but they never got his body. There was the case of Baxter also, who vanished, though his engine and some of the iron fixings were found in a wood in Leicestershire. In that case, Dr. Middleton, of Amesbury, who was watching the flight with a telescope, declares that just before the clouds obscured the view he saw the machine, which was at an enormous height, suddenly rise perpendicularly upwards in a succession of jerks in a manner that he would have thought to be impossible. That was the last seen of Baxter. There was a correspondence in the papers, but it never led to anything. There were several other similar cases, and then there was the death of Hay Connor. What a cackle there was about an unsolved mystery of the air, and what columns in the halfpenny papers, and yet how little was ever done to get to the bottom of the business! He came down in a tremendous vol-plané from an unknown height. He never got off his machine and died in his pilot's seat. Died of what? 'Heart disease,' said the doctors. Rubbish! Hay Connor's heart was as sound as mine is. What did

Venables say? Venables was the only man who was at his side when he died. He said that he was shivering and looked like a man who had been badly scared. 'Died of fright,' said Venables, but could not imagine what he was frightened about. Only said one word to Venables, which sounded like 'Monstrous.' They could make nothing of that at the inquest. But I could make something of it. Monsters! That was the last word of poor Harry Hay Connor. And he *did* die of fright, just as Venables thought.

"And then there was Myrtle's head. Do you really believe — does anybody really believe — that a man's head could be driven clean into his body by the force of a fall? Well, perhaps it may be possible, but I, for one, have never believed that it was so with Myrtle. And the grease upon his clothes — 'all slimy with grease,' said somebody at the inquest. Queer that nobody got thinking after that! I did — but, then, I had been thinking for a good long time. I've made three ascents — how Dangerfield used to chaff me about my shot-gun! — but I've never been high enough. Now, with this new light Paul Veroner machine and its one hundred and seventy-five Robur, I should easily touch the thirty thousand to-morrow. I'll have a shot at the record. Maybe I shall have a shot at something else as well. Of course, it's dangerous. If a fellow wants to avoid danger he had best keep out of flying altogether and subside finally into flannel slippers and a dressing-gown. But I'll visit the air-jungle to-morrow — and if there's anything there I shall know it. If I return, I'll find myself a bit of a celebrity. If I don't, this note-book may explain what I am trying to do, and how I lost my life in doing it. But no drivel about accidents or mysteries, if *you* please.

"I chose my Paul Veroner monoplane for the job. There's nothing like a monoplane when real work is to be done. Beaumont found that out in very early days. For one thing, it doesn't mind damp, and the weather looks as if we should be in the clouds all the time. It's a bonny little model and answers my hand like a tender-mouthed horse. The engine is a ten-cylinder rotary Robur working up to one hundred and seventy-five. It has all the modern improvements — enclosed fuselage, high-curved landing skids, brakes, gyroscopic steadiers, and three speeds, worked by an alteration of the angle of the planes upon the Venetian-blind principle. I took a shot-gun with me and a dozen cartridges filled with buck-shot. You should have seen the face of Perkins, my old mechanic, when I directed him to put them in. I was dressed like an Arctic explorer, with two jerseys under my overalls, thick socks inside my padded boots, a storm-cap with flaps, and my talc goggles. It was stifling outside the hangars, but I was going for the summit of the Himalayas, and had to dress for the part. Perkins knew there was something on and implored me to take him with me. Perhaps I should if I were using the biplane, but a monoplane is a one-man show — if you want to get the last foot of lift out of it. Of course, I took an oxygen bag; the man who goes for the altitude record without one will either be frozen or smothered — or both.

"I had a good look at the planes, the rudder-bar, and the elevating lever before I got in. Everything was in order so far as I could see. Then I switched on my engine and found that she was running sweetly. When they let her go she rose almost at once upon the lowest speed. I circled my home field once or twice just to warm her up, and then, with a wave to Perkins and the others, I flattened out my planes and put her on her highest. She skimmed like a swallow down wind for eight or ten miles until I turned her nose up a little and she began to climb in a great spiral for the cloud-bank above me. It's all-important to rise slowly and adapt yourself to the pressure as you go.

"It was a close, warm day for an English September, and there was the hush and heaviness of impending rain. Now and then there came sudden puffs of wind from the south-west — one of them so gusty and unexpected that it caught me napping and turned me half-round for an instant. I remember the time when gusts and whirls and air-pockets used to be things of danger — before we learned to put an overmastering power into our engines. Just as I reached the cloud-banks, with the altimeter marking three thousand, down came the rain. My word, how it poured! It drummed upon my wings and lashed against my face, blurring my glasses so that I could hardly see. I got down on to a low speed, for it was painful to travel against it. As I got higher it became hail, and I had to turn tail to it. One of my cylinders was out of action — a dirty plug, I should imagine, but still I was rising steadily with plenty of power. After a bit the trouble passed, whatever it was, and I heard the full, deep-throated purr — the ten singing as one. That's where the beauty of our modern silencers comes in. We can at last control our engines by ear. How they squeal and squeak and sob when they are in trouble! All those cries for help were wasted in the old days, when every sound was swallowed up by the monstrous racket of the machine. If only the early aviators could come back to see the beauty and perfection of the mechanism which have been bought at the cost of their lives!

"About nine-thirty I was nearing the clouds. Down below me, all blurred and shadowed with rain, lay the vast expanse of Salisbury Plain. Half-a-dozen flying machines were doing hackwork at the thousand-foot level, looking like little black swallows against the green background. I dare say they were wondering what I was doing up in cloud-land. Suddenly a grey curtain drew across beneath me and the wet folds of vapour were swirling round my face. It was clammily cold and miserable. But I was above the hail-storm, and that was something gained. The cloud was as dark and thick as a London fog. In my anxiety to get clear, I cocked her nose up until the automatic alarm-bell rang, and I actually began to slide backwards. My sopped and dripping wings had made me heavier than I thought, but presently I was in lighter cloud, and soon had cleared the first layer. There was a second — opal-coloured and fleecy — at a great height above my head, a white unbroken ceiling above, and a dark unbroken floor below, with the monoplane labouring upwards upon a vast spiral between them. It is deadly lonely in these cloud-spaces. Once a great flight of some small water-birds went past me, flying very fast to the westwards. The quick whirr of their wings and their musical cry were cheery to my ear. I fancy that they were teal, but I am a wretched zoologist. Now that we humans have become birds we must really learn to know our brethren by sight.

"The wind down beneath me whirled and swayed the broad cloud-plain. Once a great eddy formed in it, a whirlpool of vapour, and through it, as down a funnel, I caught sight of the distant world. A large white biplane was passing at a vast depth beneath me. I fancy it was the morning mail service betwixt Bristol and London. Then the drift swirled inwards again and the great solitude was unbroken.

"Just after ten I touched the lower edge of the upper cloud-stratum. It consisted of fine diaphanous vapour drifting swiftly from the westward. The wind had been steadily rising all this time and it was now blowing a sharp breeze — twenty-eight an hour by my gauge. Already it was very cold, though my altimeter only marked nine thousand. The engines were working beautifully, and we went droning steadily upwards. The cloud-bank was thicker than I had expected, but at last it thinned out into a golden mist before me, and then in an instant I had shot out from it, and there was an unclouded sky and a brilliant sun above my head — all blue and gold above, all shining silver below, one vast glimmering plain as far as my eyes could reach. It was a quarter past ten o'clock, and the barograph needle pointed to twelve thousand eight hundred. Up I went and up, my ears concentrated upon the deep purring of my motor, my eyes busy always with the watch, the revolution indicator, the petrol lever, and the oil pump. No wonder aviators are said to be a fearless race. With so many things to think of there is no time to trouble about oneself. About this time I noted how unreliable is the compass when above a certain height from earth. At fifteen thousand feet mine was pointing east and a point south. The sun and the wind gave me my true bearings.

"I had hoped to reach an eternal stillness in these high altitudes, but with every thousand feet of ascent the gale grew stronger. My machine groaned and trembled in every joint and rivet as she faced it, and swept away like a sheet of paper when I banked her on the turn, skimming down wind at a greater pace, perhaps, than ever mortal man has moved. Yet I had always to turn again and tack up in the wind's eye, for it was not merely a height record that I was after. By all my calculations it was above little Wiltshire that my air-jungle lay, and all my labour might be lost if I struck the outer layers at some farther point.

"When I reached the nineteen-thousand-foot level, which was about midday, the wind was so severe that I looked with some anxiety to the stays of my wings, expecting momentarily to see them snap or slacken. I even cast loose the parachute behind me, and fastened its hook into the ring of my leathern belt, so as to be ready for the worst. Now was the time when a bit of scamped work by the mechanic is paid for by the life of the aeronaut. But she held together bravely. Every cord and strut was humming and vibrating like so many harp-strings, but it was glorious to see how, for all the beating and the buffeting, she was still the conqueror of Nature and the mistress of the sky. There is surely something divine in man himself that he should rise so superior to the limitations which Creation seemed to impose — rise, too, by such unselfish, heroic devotion as this air-conquest has shown. Talk of human degeneration! When has such a story as this been written in the annals of our race?

"These were the thoughts in my head as I climbed that monstrous inclined plane with the wind sometimes beating in my face and sometimes whistling behind my ears, while the cloud-land beneath me fell away to such a distance that the folds and hummocks of silver had all smoothed out into one flat, shining plain. But suddenly I had a horrible and unprecedented experience. I have known before what it is to be in what our neighbours have called a *tourbillon*, but never on such a scale as this. That huge, sweeping river of wind of which I have spoken had, as it appears, whirlpools within it which were as monstrous as itself. Without a moment's warning I was dragged suddenly into the heart of one. I spun round for a minute or two with such velocity that I almost lost my senses, and then fell suddenly, left wing foremost, down the vacuum funnel in the centre. I dropped like a stone, and lost nearly a thousand feet. It was only my belt that kept me in my seat, and the shock and breathlessness left me hanging half-insensible over the side of the fuselage. But I am always capable of a supreme effort — it is my one great merit as an aviator. I was conscious that the descent was slower. The whirlpool was a cone rather than a funnel, and I had come to the apex. With a terrific wrench, throwing my weight all to one side, I levelled my planes and brought her head away from the wind. In an instant I had shot out of the eddies and was skimming down the sky. Then, shaken but victorious, I turned her nose up and began once more my steady grind on the upward spiral. I took a large sweep to avoid the danger-spot of the whirlpool, and soon I was safely above it. Just after one o'clock I was twenty-one thousand feet above the sea-level. To my great joy I had topped the gale, and with every hundred feet of ascent the air grew stiller. On the other hand, it was very cold, and I was conscious of that peculiar nausea which goes with rarefaction of the air. For the first time I unscrewed the mouth of my oxygen bag and took an occasional whiff of the glorious gas. I could feel it running like a cordial through my veins, and I was exhilarated almost to the point of drunkenness. I shouted and sang as I soared upwards into the cold, still outer world.

"It is very clear to me that the insensibility which came upon Glaisher, and in a lesser degree upon Coxwell, when, in 1862, they ascended in a balloon to the height of thirty thousand feet, was due to the extreme speed with which a perpendicular ascent is made. Doing it at an easy gradient and ac-customing oneself to the lessened barometric pres-sure by slow degrees, there are no such dreadful symptoms. At the same great height I found that even without my oxygen inhaler I could breathe without undue distress. It was bitterly cold, how-ever, and my thermometer was at zero Fahrenheit. At one-thirty I was nearly seven miles above the surface of the earth, and still ascending steadily. I found, however, that the rarefied air was giving markedly less support to my planes, and that my angle of ascent had to be considerably lowered in consequence. It was already clear that even with my light weight and strong engine-power there was a point in front of me where I should be held. To make matters worse, one of my sparking-plugs was in trouble again and there was intermittent missfiring in the engine. My heart was heavy with the fear of failure.

"It was about that time that I had a most extraordinary experience. Something whizzed past me in a trail of smoke and exploded with a loud, hissing sound, sending forth a cloud of steam. For the instant I could not imagine what had happened. Then I remembered that the earth is for ever being bombarded by meteor stones, and would be hardly inhabitable were they not in nearly every case turned to vapour in the outer layers of the atmosphere. Here is a new danger for the high-altitude man, for two others passed me when I was nearing the forty-thousand-foot mark. I cannot doubt that at the edge of the earth's envelope the risk would be a very real one.

"My barograph needle marked forty-one thousand three hundred when I became aware that I could go no farther. Physically, the strain was not as yet greater than I could bear, but my machine had reached its limit. The attenuated air gave no firm support to the wings, and the least tilt developed into side-slip, while she seemed sluggish on her controls. Possibly, had the engine been at its best, another thousand feet might have been within our capacity, but it was still missfiring, and two out of the ten cylinders appeared to be out of action. If I had not already reached the zone for which I was searching then I should never see it upon this journey. But was it not possible that I had attained it? Soaring in circles like a monstrous hawk upon the forty-thousand-foot level I let the monoplane guide herself, and with my Mannheim glass I made a careful observation of my surroundings. The heavens were perfectly clear; there was no indication of those dangers which I had imagined.

"I have said that I was soaring in circles. It struck me suddenly that I would do well to take a wider sweep and open up a new air-tract. If the hunter entered an earth-jungle he would drive through it if he wished to find his game. My reasoning had led me to believe that the air-jungle which I had imagined lay somewhere over Wiltshire. This should be to the south and west of me. I took my bearings from the sun, for the compass was hopeless and no trace of earth was to be seen — nothing but the distant silver cloud-plain. However, I got my direction as best I might and kept her head straight to the mark. I reckoned that my petrol supply would not last for more than another hour or so, but I could afford to use it to the last drop, since a single magnificent vol-plané could at any time take me to the earth.

"Suddenly I was aware of something new. The air in front of me had lost its crystal clearness. It was full of long, ragged wisps of something which I can only compare to very fine cigarette-smoke. It hung about in wreaths and coils, turning and twisting slowly in the sunlight. As the monoplane shot through it, I was aware of a faint taste of oil upon my lips, and there was a greasy scum upon the wood-work of the machine. Some infinitely fine organic matter appeared to be suspended in the atmosphere. There was no life there. It was inchoate and diffuse, extending for many square acres and then fringing off into the void. No, it was not life. But might it not be the remains of life? Above all, might it not be the food of life, of monstrous life, even as the humble grease of the ocean is the food for the mighty whale? The thought was in my mind when my eyes looked upwards and I saw the most wonderful vision that ever man has seen. Can I hope to convey it to you even as I saw it myself last Thursday?

"Conceive a jelly-fish such as sails in our sum-mer seas, bell-shaped and of enormous size — far larger, I should judge, than the dome of St. Paul's. It was of a light pink colour veined with a delicate green, but the whole huge fabric so tenuous that it was but a fairy outline against the dark blue sky. It pulsated with a delicate and regular rhythm. From it there depended two long, drooping green tentacles, which swayed slowly backwards and forwards. This gorgeous vision passed gently with noiseless dignity over my head, as light and fragile as a soap-bubble, and drifted upon its stately way.

"I had half-turned my monoplane, that I might look after this beautiful creature, when, in a moment, I found myself amidst a perfect fleet of them, of all sizes, but none so large as the first. Some were quite small, but the majority about as big as an average balloon, and with much the same curvature at the top. There was in them a delicacy of texture and colouring which reminded me of the finest Venetian glass. Pale shades of pink and green were the prevailing tints, but all had a lovely iridescence where the sun shimmered through their dainty forms. Some hundreds of them drifted past me, a wonderful fairy squadron of strange, unknown argosies of the sky — creatures whose forms and substance were so attuned to these pure heights that one could not conceive anything so delicate within actual sight or sound of earth.

"But soon my attention was drawn to a new phenomenon — the serpents of the outer air. These were long, thin, fantastic coils of vapour-like material, which turned and twisted with great speed, flying round and round at such a pace that the eyes could hardly follow them. Some of these ghost-like creatures were twenty or thirty feet long, but it was difficult to tell their girth, for their outline was so hazy that it seemed to fade away into the air around them. These air-snakes were of a very light grey or smoke colour, with some darker lines within, which gave the impression of a definite organism. One of them whisked past my very face, and I was conscious of a cold, clammy contact, but their composition was so unsubstantial that I could not connect them with any thought of physical danger, any more than the beautiful bell-like creatures which had preceded them. There was no more solidity in their frames than in the floating spume from a broken wave.

"But a more terrible experience was in store for me. Floating downwards from a great height there came a purplish patch of vapour, small as I saw it first, but rapidly enlarging as it approached me, until it appeared to be hundreds of square feet in size. Though fashioned of some transparent, jelly-like substance, it was none the less of much more definite outline and solid consistence than anything which I had seen before. There were more traces, too, of a physical organization, especially two vast shadowy, circular plates upon either side, which may have been eyes, and a perfectly solid white projection between them which was as curved and cruel as the beak of a vulture.

"The whole aspect of this monster was formidable and threatening, and it kept changing its colour from a very light mauve to a dark, angry purple so thick that it cast a shadow as it drifted between my monoplane and the sun. On the upper curve of its huge body there were three great projections which I can only describe as enormous bubbles, and I was convinced as I looked at them that they were charged with some extremely light gas which served to buoy-up the misshapen and semi-solid mass in the rarefied air. The creature moved swiftly along, keeping pace easily with the monoplane, and for twenty miles or more it formed my horrible escort, hovering over me like a bird of prey which is waiting to pounce. Its method of progression — done so swiftly that it was not easy to follow — was to throw out a long, glutinous streamer in front of it, which in turn seemed to draw forward the rest of the writhing body. So elastic and gelatinous was it that never for two successive minutes was it the same shape, and yet each change made it more threatening and loathsome than the last.

"I knew that it meant mischief. Every purple flush of its hideous body told me so. The vague, goggling eyes which were turned always upon me were cold and merciless in their viscid hatred. I dipped the nose of my monoplane downwards to escape it. As I did so, as quick as a flash there shot out a long tentacle from this mass of floating blubber, and it fell as light and sinuous as a whip-lash across the front of my machine. There was a loud hiss as it lay for a moment across the hot engine, and it whisked itself into the air again, while the huge flat body drew itself together as if in sudden pain. I dipped to a vol-piqué, but again a tentacle fell over the monoplane and was shorn off by the propeller as easily as it might have cut through a smoke wreath. A long, gliding, sticky, serpent-like coil came from behind and caught me round the waist, dragging me out of the fuselage. I tore at it, my fingers sinking into the smooth, glue-like surface, and for an instant I disengaged myself, but only to be caught round the boot by another coil, which gave me a jerk that tilted me almost on to my back.

"As I fell over I blazed off both barrels of my gun, though, indeed, it was like attacking an elephant with a pea-shooter to imagine that any human weapon could cripple that mighty bulk. And yet I aimed better than I knew, for, with a loud report, one of the great blisters upon the creature's back exploded with the puncture of the buck-shot. It was very clear that my conjecture was right, and that these vast clear bladders were distended with some lifting gas, for in an instant the huge cloud-like body turned sideways, writhing desperately to find its balance, while the white beak snapped and gaped in horrible fury. But already I had shot away on the steepest glide that I dared to attempt, my engine still full on, the flying propeller and the force of gravity shooting me downwards like an aerolite. Far behind me I saw a dull, purplish smudge growing swiftly smaller and merging into the blue sky behind it. I was safe out of the deadly jungle of the outer air.

"Once out of danger I throttled my engine, for nothing tears a machine to pieces quicker than running on full power from a height. It was a glorious spiral vol-plané from nearly eight miles of altitude — first, to the level of the silver cloud-bank, then to that of the storm-cloud beneath it, and finally, in beating rain, to the surface of the earth. I saw the Bristol Channel beneath me as I broke from the clouds, but, having still some petrol in my tank, I got twenty miles inland before I found myself stranded in a field half a mile from the village of Ashcombe. There I got three tins of petrol from a passing motor-car, and at ten minutes past six that evening I alighted gently in my own home meadow at Devizes, after such a journey as no mortal upon earth has ever yet taken and lived to tell the tale. I have seen the beauty and I have seen the horror of the heights — and greater beauty or greater horror than that is not within the ken of man.

"And now it is my plan to go once again before I give my results to the world. My reason for this is that I must surely have something to show by way of proof before I lay such a tale before my fellow-men. It is true that others will soon follow and will confirm what I have said, and yet I should wish to carry conviction from the first. Those lovely iridescent bubbles of the air should not be hard to capture. They drift slowly upon their way, and the swift monoplane could intercept their leisurely course. It is likely enough that they would dissolve in the heavier layers of the atmosphere, and that some small heap of amorphous jelly might be all that I should bring to earth with me. And yet something there would surely be by which I could substantiate my story. Yes, I will go, even if I run a risk by doing so. These purple horrors would not seem to be numerous. It is probable that I shall not see one. If I do I shall dive at once. At the worst there is always the shot-gun and my knowledge of . . ."

Here a page of the manuscript is unfortunately missing. On the next page is written, in large, straggling writing: —

"Forty-three thousand feet. I shall never see earth again. They are beneath me, three of them. God help me; it is a dreadful death to die!"

Such in its entirety is the Joyce-Armstrong Statement. Of the man nothing has since been seen. Pieces of his shattered monoplane have been picked up in the preserves of Mr. Budd-Lushington upon the borders of Kent and Sussex, within a few miles of the spot where the note-book was discovered. If the unfortunate aviator's theory is correct that this air-jungle, as he called it, existed only over the south-west of England, then it would seem that he had fled from it at the full speed of his monoplane, but had been overtaken and devoured by these horrible creatures at some spot in the outer atmosphere above the place where the grim relics were found. The picture of that monoplane skimming down the sky, with the nameless terrors flying as swiftly beneath it and cutting it off always from the earth while they gradually closed in upon their victim, is one upon which a man who valued his sanity would prefer not to dwell. There are many, as I am aware, who still jeer at the facts which I have here set down, but even they must admit that Joyce-Armstrong has disappeared, and I would commend to them his own words: "This note-book may explain what I am trying to do, and how I lost my life in doing it. But no drivel about accidents or mysteries, if *you* please."

VI. BORROWED SCENES

"It cannot be done. People really would not stand it. I know because I have tried." — *Extract from an unpublished paper upon George Borrow and his writings.*

Yes, I tried and my experience may interest other people. You must imagine, then, that I am soaked in George Borrow, especially in his *Lavengro* and his *Romany Rye*, that I have modelled both my thoughts, my speech and my style very carefully upon those of the master, and that finally I set forth one summer day actually to lead the life of which I had read. Behold me, then, upon the country road which leads from the railway-station to the Sussex village of Swinehurst.

As I walked, I entertained myself by recollections of the founders of Sussex, of Cerdic that mighty sea-rover, and of Ella his son, said by the bard to be taller by the length of a spear-head than the tallest of his fellows. I mentioned the matter twice to peasants whom I met upon the road. One, a tallish man with a freckled face, sidled past me and ran swiftly towards the station. The other, a smaller and older man, stood entranced while I recited to him that passage of the Saxon Chronicle which begins, "Then came Leija with longships forty-four, and the fyrd went out against him." I was pointing out to him that the Chronicle had been written partly by the monks of Saint Albans and afterwards by those of Peterborough, but the fellow sprang suddenly over a gate and disappeared.

The village of Swinehurst is a straggling line of half-timbered houses of the early English pattern. One of these houses stood, as I observed, somewhat taller than the rest, and seeing by its appearance and by the sign which hung before it that it was the village inn, I approached it, for indeed I had not broken my fast since I had left London. A stoutish man, five foot eight perhaps in height, with black coat and trousers of a greyish shade, stood outside, and to him I talked in the fashion of the master.

"Why a rose and why a crown?" I asked as I pointed upwards.

He looked at me in a strange manner. The man's whole appearance was strange. "Why not?" he answered, and shrank a little backwards.

"The sign of a king," said I.

"Surely," said he. "What else should we understand from a crown?"

"And which king?" I asked.

"You will excuse me," said he, and tried to pass.

"Which king?" I repeated.

"How should I know?" he asked.

"You should know by the rose," said I, "which is the symbol of that Tudor-ap-Tudor, who, coming from the mountains of Wales, yet seated his posterity upon the English throne. Tudor," I continued, getting between the stranger and the door of the inn, through which he appeared to be desirous of passing, "was of the same blood as Owen Glendower, the famous chieftain, who is by no means to be confused with Owen Gwynedd, the father of Madoc of the Sea, of whom the bard made the famous cnylyn, which runs in the Welsh as follows: — "

I was about to repeat the famous stanza of Dafydd-ap-Gwilyn when the man, who had looked very fixedly and strangely at me as I spoke, pushed past me and entered the inn. "Truly," said I aloud, "it is surely Swinehurst to which I have come, since the same means the grove of the hogs." So saying I followed the fellow into the bar parlour, where I perceived him seated in a corner with a large chair in front of him. Four persons of various degrees were drinking beer at a central table, whilst a small man of active build, in a black, shiny suit, which seemed to have seen much service, stood before the empty fireplace. Him I took to be the landlord, and I asked him what I should have for my dinner.

He smiled, and said that he could not tell.

"But surely, my friend," said I, "you can tell me what is ready?"

"Even that I cannot do," he answered; "but I doubt not that the landlord can inform us." On this he rang the bell, and a fellow answered, to whom I put the same question.

"What would you have?" he asked.

I thought of the master, and I ordered a cold leg of pork to be washed down with tea and beer.

"Did you say tea *and* beer?" asked the landlord.

"I did."

"For twenty-five years have I been in business," said the landlord, "and never before have I been asked for tea and beer."

"The gentleman is joking," said the man with the shining coat.

"Or else — " said the elderly man in the corner.

"Or what, sir?" I asked.

"Nothing," said he — "nothing." There was something very strange in this man in the corner — him to whom I had spoken of Dafydd-ap-Gwilyn.

"Then you are joking," said the landlord.

I asked him if he had read the works of my master, George Borrow. He said that he had not. I told him that in those five volumes he would not, from cover to cover, find one trace of any sort of a joke. He would also find that my master drank tea and beer together. Now it happens that about tea I have read nothing either in the sagas or in the bardic cnylynions, but, whilst the landlord had departed to prepare my meal, I recited to the company those Icelandic stanzas which praise the beer of Gunnar, the long-haired son of Harold the Bear. Then, lest the language should be unknown to some of them, I recited my own translation, ending with the line —

If the beer be small, then let the mug be large.

I then asked the company whether they went to church or to chapel. The question surprised them, and especially the strange man in the corner, upon whom I now fixed my eye. I had read his secret, and as I looked at him he tried to shrink behind the clock-case.

"The church or the chapel?" I asked him.

"The church," he gasped.

"*Which* church?" I asked.

He shrank farther behind the clock. "I have never been so questioned," he cried.

I showed him that I knew his secret, "Rome was not built in a day," said I.

"He! He!" he cried. Then, as I turned away, he put his head from behind the clock-case and tapped his forehead with his forefinger. So also did the man with the shiny coat, who stood before the empty fireplace.

Having eaten the cold leg of pork — where is there a better dish, save only boiled mutton with capers? — and having drunk both the tea and the beer, I told the company that such a meal had been called "to box Harry" by the master, who had observed it to be in great favour with commercial gentlemen out of Liverpool. With this information and a stanza or two from Lopez de Vega I left the Inn of the Rose and Crown behind me, having first paid my reckoning. At the door the landlord asked me for my name and address.

"And why?" I asked.

"Lest there should be inquiry for you," said the landlord.

"But why should they inquire for me?"

"Ah, who knows?" said the landlord, musing. And so I left him at the door of the Inn of the Rose and Crown, whence came, I observed, a great tumult of laughter. "Assuredly," thought I, "Rome was not built in a day."

Having walked down the main street of Swine-hurst, which, as I have observed, consists of half-timbered buildings in the ancient style, I came out upon the country road, and proceeded to look for those wayside adventures, which are, according to the master, as thick as blackberries for those who seek them upon an English highway. I had already received some boxing lessons before leaving London, so it seemed to me that if I should chance to meet some traveller whose size and age seemed such as to encourage the venture I would ask him to strip off his coat and settle any differences which we could find in the old English fashion. I waited, therefore, by a stile for any one who should chance to pass, and it was while I stood there that the screaming horror came upon me, even as it came upon the master in the dingle. I gripped the bar of the stile, which was of good British oak. Oh, who can tell the terrors of the screaming horror! That was what I thought as I grasped the oaken bar of the stile. Was it the beer — or was it the tea? Or was it that the landlord was right and that other, the man with the black, shiny coat, he who had answered the sign of the strange man in the corner? But the master drank tea with beer. Yes, but the master also had the screaming horror. All this I thought as I grasped the bar of British oak, which was the top of the stile. For half an hour the horror was upon me. Then it passed, and I was left feeling very weak and still grasping the oaken bar.

I had not moved from the stile, where I had been seized by the screaming horror, when I heard the sound of steps behind me, and turning round I perceived that a pathway led across the field upon the farther side of the stile. A woman was coming towards me along this pathway, and it was evident to me that she was one of those gipsy Rias, of whom the master has said so much. Looking beyond her, I could see the smoke of a fire from a small dingle, which showed where her tribe were camping. The woman herself was of a moderate height, neither tall nor short, with a face which was much sunburned and freckled. I must confess that she was not beautiful, but I do not think that anyone, save the master, has found very beautiful women walking about upon the high-roads of England. Such as she was I must make the best of her, and well I knew how to address her, for many times had I admired the mixture of politeness and audacity which should be used in such a case. Therefore, when the woman had come to the stile, I held out my hand and helped her over.

"What says the Spanish poet Calderon?" said I. "I doubt not that you have read the couplet which has been thus Englished:

Oh, maiden, may I humbly pray
That I may help you on your way."

The woman blushed, but said nothing.

"Where," I asked, "are the Romany chals and

the Romany chis?"

She turned her head away and was silent.

"Though I am a gorgio," said I, "I know something of the Romany lil," and to prove it I sang the stanza —

Coliko, coliko saulo wer
Apopli to the farming ker
Will wel and mang him mullo,
Will wel and mang his truppo.

The girl laughed, but said nothing. It appeared to me from her appearance that she might be one of those who make a living at telling fortunes or "dukkering," as the master calls it, at racecourses and other gatherings of the sort.

"Do you dukker?" I asked.

She slapped me on the arm. "Well, you *are* a pot of ginger!" said she.

I was pleased at the slap, for it put me in mind of the peerless Belle. "You can use Long Melford," said I, an expression which, with the master, meant fighting.

"Get along with your sauce!" said she, and struck me again.

"You are a very fine young woman," said I, "and remind me of Grunelda, the daughter of Hjalmar, who stole the golden bowl from the King of the Islands."

She seemed annoyed at this. "You keep a civil tongue, young man," said she.

"I meant no harm, Belle. I was but comparing you to one of whom the saga says her eyes were like the shine of sun upon icebergs."

This seemed to please her, for she smiled. "My name ain't Belle," she said at last.

"What is your name?"

"Henrietta."

"The name of a queen," I said aloud.

"Go on," said the girl.

"Of Charles's queen," said I, "of whom Waller the poet (for the English also have their poets, though in this respect far inferior to the Basques) — of whom, I say, Waller the poet said:

That she was Queen was the Creator's act,
Belated man could but endorse the fact."

"I say!" cried the girl. "How you do go on!"

"So now," said I, "since I have shown you that you are a queen you will surely give me a choomer" — this being a kiss in Romany talk.

"I'll give you one on the ear-hole," she cried.

"Then I will wrestle with you," said I. "If you should chance to put me down, I will do penance by teaching you the Armenian alphabet — the very word alphabet, as you will perceive, shows us that our letters came from Greece. If, on the other hand, I should chance to put you down, you will give me a choomer."

I had got so far, and she was climbing the stile

with some pretence of getting away from me, when there came a van along the road, belonging, as I discovered, to a baker in Swinehurst. The horse, which was of a brown colour, was such as is bred in the New Forest, being somewhat under fifteen hands and of a hairy, ill-kempt variety. As I know less than the master about horses, I will say no more of this horse, save to repeat that its colour was brown — nor indeed had the horse or the horse's colour anything to do with my narrative. I might add, however, that it could either be taken as a small horse or as a large pony, being somewhat tall for the one, but undersized for the other. I have now said enough about this horse, which has nothing to do with my story, and I will turn my attention to the driver.

This was a man with a broad, florid face and brown side-whiskers. He was of a stout build and had rounded shoulders, with a small mole of a reddish colour over his left eyebrow. His jacket was of velveteen, and he had large, iron-shod boots, which were perched upon the splashboard in front of him. He pulled up the van as he came up to the stile near which I was standing with the maiden who had come from the dingle, and in a civil fashion he asked me if I could oblige him with a light for his pipe. Then, as I drew a matchbox from my pocket, he threw his reins over the splashboard, and removing his large, iron-shod boots he descended on to the road. He was a burly man, but inclined to fat and scant of breath. It seemed to me that it was a chance for one of those wayside boxing adventures which were so common in the olden times. It was my intention that I should fight the man, and that the maiden from the dingle standing by me should tell me when to use my right or my left, as the case might be, picking me up also in case I should be so unfortunate as to be knocked down by the man with the iron-shod boots and the small mole of a reddish colour over his left eyebrow.

"Do you use Long Melford?" I asked.

He looked at me in some surprise, and said that any mixture was good enough for him.

"By Long Melford," said I, "I do not mean, as you seem to think, some form of tobacco, but I mean that art and science of boxing which was held in such high esteem by our ancestors, that some famous professors of it, such as the great Gully, have been elected to the highest offices of the State. There were men of the highest character amongst the bruisers of England, of whom I would particularly mention Tom of Hereford, better known as Tom Spring, though his father's name, as I have been given to understand, was Winter. This, however, has nothing to do with the matter in hand, which is that you must fight me."

The man with the florid face seemed very much surprised at my words, so that I cannot think that adventures of this sort were as common as I had been led by the master to expect.

"Fight!" said he. "What about?"

"It is a good old English custom," said I, "by which we may determine which is the better man."

"I've nothing against you," said he.

"Nor I against you," I answered. "So that we will fight for love, which was an expression much used in olden days. It is narrated by Harold Sygvynson that among the Danes it was usual to do so even with battle-axes, as is told in his second set of runes. Therefore you will take off your coat and fight." As I spoke, I stripped off my own.

The man's face was less florid than before. "I'm not going to fight," said he.

"Indeed you are," I answered, "and this young woman will doubtless do you the service to hold your coat."

"You're clean balmy," said Henrietta.

"Besides," said I, "if you will not fight me for love, perhaps you will fight me for this," and I held out a sovereign. "Will you hold his coat?" I said to Henrietta.

"I'll hold the thick 'un," said she.

"No, you don't," said the man, and put the sovereign into the pocket of his trousers, which were of a corduroy material. "Now," said he, "what am I to do to earn this?"

"Fight," said I.

"How do you do it?" he asked.

"Put up your hands," I answered.

He put them up as I had said, and stood there in a sheepish manner with no idea of anything further. It seemed to me that if I could make him angry he would do better, so I knocked off his hat, which was black and hard, of the kind which is called billy-cock.

"Heh, guv'nor!" he cried, "what are you up to?"

"That was to make you angry," said I.

"Well, I am angry," said he.

"Then here is your hat," said I, "and afterwards we shall fight."

I turned as I spoke to pick up his hat, which had rolled behind where I was standing. As I stooped to reach it, I received such a blow that I could neither rise erect nor yet sit down. This blow which I received as I stooped for his billy-cock hat was not from his fist, but from his iron-shod boot, the same which I had observed upon the splashboard. Being unable either to rise erect or yet to sit down, I leaned upon the oaken bar of the stile and groaned loudly on account of the pain of the blow which I had received. Even the screaming horror had given me less pain than this blow from the iron-shod boot. When at last I was able to stand erect, I found that the florid-faced man had driven away with his cart, which could no longer be seen. The maiden from the dingle was standing at the other side of the stile, and a ragged man was running across the field from the direction of the fire.

"Why did you not warn me, Henrietta?" I asked.

"I hadn't time," said she. "Why were you such a chump as to turn your back on him like that?"

The ragged man had reached us, where I stood

talking to Henrietta by the stile. I will not try to write his conversation as he said it, because I have observed that the master never condescends to dialect, but prefers by a word introduced here and there to show the fashion of a man's speech. I will only say that the man from the dingle spoke as did the Anglo-Saxons, who were wont, as is clearly shown by the venerable Bede, to call their leaders 'Enjist and 'Orsa, two words which in their proper meaning signify a horse and a mare.

"What did he hit you for?" asked the man from the dingle. He was exceedingly ragged, with a powerful frame, a lean brown face, and an oaken cudgel in his hand. His voice was very hoarse and rough, as is the case with those who live in the open air. "The bloke hit you," said he. "What did the bloke hit you for?"

"He asked him to," said Henrietta.

"Asked him to — asked him what?"

"Why, he asked him to hit him. Gave him a thick 'un to do it."

The ragged man seemed surprised. "See here, gov'nor," said he. "If you're collectin', I could let you have one half-price."

"He took me unawares," said I.

"What else would the bloke do when you bashed his hat?" said the maiden from the dingle.

By this time I was able to straighten myself up by the aid of the oaken bar which formed the top of the stile. Having quoted a few lines of the Chinese poet Lo-tun-an to the effect that, however hard a knock might be, it might always conceivably be harder, I looked about for my coat, but could by no means find it.

"Henrietta," I said, "what have you done with my coat?"

"Look here, gov'nor," said the man from the dingle, "not so much Henrietta, if it's the same to you. This woman's my wife. Who are you to call her Henrietta?"

I assured the man from the dingle that I had meant no disrespect to his wife. "I had thought she was a mort," said I; "but the ria of a Romany chal is always sacred to me."

"Clean balmy," said the woman.

"Some other day," said I, "I may visit you in your camp in the dingle and read you the master's book about the Romanys."

"What's Romanys?" asked the man.

Myself. Romanys are gipsies.

The Man. We ain't gipsies.

Myself. What are you then?

The Man. We are hoppers.

Myself (to Henrietta). Then how did you understand all I have said to you about gipsies?

Henrietta. I didn't.

I again asked for my coat, but it was clear now

that before offering to fight the florid-faced man with the mole over his left eyebrow I must have hung my coat upon the splashboard of his van. I therefore recited a verse from Ferideddin-Atar, the Persian poet, which signifies that it is more important to preserve your skin than your clothes, and bidding farewell to the man from the dingle and his wife I returned into the old English village of Swinehurst, where I was able to buy a second-hand coat, which enabled me to make my way to the station, where I should start for London. I could not but remark with some surprise that I was followed to the station by many of the villagers, together with the man with the shiny coat, and that other, the strange man, he who had slunk behind the clock-case. From time to time I turned and approached them, hoping to fall into conversation with them; but as I did so they would break and hasten down the road. Only the village constable came on, and he walked by my side and listened while I told him the history of Hunyadi Janos and the events which occurred during the wars between that hero, known also as Corvinus or the crow-like, and Mahommed the second, he who captured Constantinople, better known as Byzantium, before the Christian epoch. Together with the constable I entered the station, and seating myself in a carriage I took paper from my pocket and I began to write upon the paper all that had occurred to me, in order that I might show that it was not easy in these days to follow the example of the master. As I wrote, I heard the constable talk to the station-master, a stout, middle-sized man with a red neck-tie, and tell him of my own adventures in the old English village of Swinehurst.

"He is a gentleman too," said the constable, "and I doubt not that he lives in a big house in London town."

"A very big house if every man had his rights," said the station-master, and waving his hand he signalled that the train should proceed.

VII. THE SURGEON OF GASTER FELL

I — HOW THE WOMAN CAME TO KIRKBY-MALHOUSE

Bleak and wind-swept is the little town of Kirkby-Malhouse, harsh and forbidding are the fells upon which it stands. It stretches in a single line of grey-stone, slate-roofed houses, dotted down the furze-clad slope of the rolling moor.

In this lonely and secluded village, I, James Upperton, found myself in the summer of '85. Little as the hamlet had to offer, it contained that for which I yearned above all things — seclusion and freedom from all which might distract my mind from the high and weighty subjects which engaged it. But the inquisitiveness of my landlady made my lodgings undesirable and I determined to seek new quarters.

As it chanced, I had in one of my rambles come upon an isolated dwelling in the very heart of these lonely moors, which I at once determined should be my own. It was a two-roomed cottage, which had once belonged to some shepherd, but had long been deserted, and was crumbling rapidly to ruin. In the winter floods, the Gaster Beck, which runs down Gaster Fell, where the little dwelling stood, had overswept its banks and torn away a part of the wall. The roof was in ill case, and the scattered slates lay thick amongst the grass. Yet the main shell of the house stood firm and true; and it was no great task for me to have all that was amiss set right.

The two rooms I laid out in a widely different manner — my own tastes are of a Spartan turn, and the outer chamber was so planned as to accord with them. An oil-stove by Rippingille of Birmingham furnished me with the means of cooking; while two great bags, the one of flour, and the other of potatoes, made me independent of all supplies from without. In diet I had long been a Pythagorean, so that the scraggy, long-limbed sheep which browsed upon the wiry grass by the Gaster Beck had little to fear from their new companion. A nine-gallon cask of oil served me as a sideboard; while a square table, a deal chair and a truckle-bed completed the list of my domestic fittings. At the head of my couch hung two unpainted shelves — the lower for my dishes and cooking utensils, the upper for the few portraits which took me back to the little that was pleasant in the long, wearisome toiling for wealth and for pleasure which had marked the life I had left behind.

If this dwelling-room of mine were plain even to squalor, its poverty was more than atoned for by the luxury of the chamber which was destined to serve me as my study. I had ever held that it was best for my mind to be surrounded by such objects as would be in harmony with the studies which occupied it, and that the loftiest and most ethereal conditions of thought are only possible amid surroundings which please the eye and gratify the senses. The room which I had set apart for my mystic studies was set forth in a style as gloomy and majestic as the thoughts and aspirations with which it was to harmonise. Both walls and ceilings were covered with a paper of the richest and glossiest black, on which was traced a lurid and arabesque pattern of dead gold. A black velvet curtain covered the single diamond-paned window; while a thick, yielding carpet of the same material prevented the sound of my own footfalls, as I paced backward and forward, from breaking the current of my thought. Along the cornices ran gold rods, from which depended six pictures, all of the sombre and imaginative caste, which chimed best with my fancy.

And yet it was destined that ere ever I reached this quiet harbour I should learn that I was still one of humankind, and that it is an ill thing to strive to break the bond which binds us to our fellows. It was but two nights before the date I had fixed upon for my change of dwelling, when I was conscious of a bustle in the house beneath, with the bearing of heavy burdens up the creaking stair, and the harsh voice of my landlady, loud in welcome and protestations of joy. From time to time, amid the whirl of words, I could hear a gentle and softly modulated voice, which struck pleasantly upon my ear after the long weeks during which I had listened only to the rude dialect of the dalesmen. For an hour I could hear the dialogue beneath — the high voice and the low, with clatter of cup and clink of spoon, until at last a light, quick step passed my study door, and I knew that my new fellow lodger had sought her room.

On the morning after this incident I was up betimes, as is my wont; but I was surprised, on glancing from my window, to see that our new inmate was earlier still. She was walking down the narrow pathway, which zigzags over the fell — a tall woman, slender, her head sunk upon her breast, her arms filled with a bristle of wild flowers, which she had gathered in her morning rambles. The white and pink of her dress, and the touch of deep red ribbon in her broad drooping hat, formed a pleasant dash of colour against the dun-tinted landscape. She was some distance off when I first set eyes upon her, yet I knew that this wandering woman could be none other than our arrival of last night, for there was a grace and refinement in her bearing which marked her from the dwellers of the fells. Even as I watched, she passed swiftly and lightly down the pathway, and turning through the wicket gate, at the further end of our cottage garden, she seated herself upon the green bank which faced my window, and strewing her flowers in front of her, set herself to arrange them.

As she sat there, with the rising sun at her back, and the glow of the morning spreading like an aureole around her stately and well-poised head, I could see that she was a woman of extraordinary personal beauty. Her face was Spanish rather than English in its type — oval, olive, with black, sparkling eyes, and a sweetly sensitive mouth. From under the broad straw hat two thick coils of blue-black hair curved down on either side of her graceful, queenly neck. I was surprised, as I watched her, to see that her shoes and skirt bore witness to a journey rather than to a mere morning ramble. Her light dress was stained, wet and bedraggled; while her boots were thick with the yellow soil of the fells. Her face, too, wore a weary expression, and her young beauty seemed to be clouded over by the shadow of inward trouble. Even as I watched her, she burst suddenly into wild weeping, and throwing down her bundle of flowers ran swiftly into the house.

Distrait as I was and weary of the ways of the world, I was conscious of a sudden pang of sympathy and grief as I looked upon the spasm of despair which, seemed to convulse this strange and beautiful woman. I bent to my books, and yet my thoughts would ever turn to her proud clear-cut face, her weather-stained dress, her drooping head, and the sorrow which lay in each line and feature of her pensive face.

Mrs. Adams, my landlady, was wont to carry up my frugal breakfast; yet it was very rarely that I allowed her to break the current of my thoughts, or to draw my mind by her idle chatter from weightier things. This morning, however, for once, she found me in a listening mood, and with little prompting, proceeded to pour into my ears all that she knew of our beautiful visitor.

"Miss Eva Cameron be her name, sir," she said: "but who she be, or where she came fra, I know little more than yoursel'. Maybe it was the same reason that brought her to Kirkby-Malhouse as fetched you there yoursel', sir."

"Possibly," said I, ignoring the covert question; "but I should hardly have thought that Kirkby-Malhouse was a place which offered any great attractions to a young lady."

"Heh, sir!" she cried, "there's the wonder of it. The leddy has just come fra France; and how her folk come to learn of me is just a wonder. A week ago, up comes a man to my door — a fine man, sir, and a gentleman, as one could see with half an eye. 'You are Mrs. Adams,' says he. 'I engage your rooms for Miss Cameron,' says he. 'She will be here in a week,' says he; and then off without a word of terms. Last night there comes the young leddy hersel' — soft-spoken and downcast, with a touch of the French in her speech. But my sakes, sir! I must away and mak' her some tea, for she'll feel lonesome-like, poor lamb, when she wakes under a strange roof."

II — HOW I WENT FORTH TO GASTER FELL

I was still engaged upon my breakfast when I heard the clatter of dishes and the landlady's footfall as she passed toward her new lodger's room. An instant afterward she had rushed down the passage and burst in upon me with uplifted hand and startled eyes. "Lord 'a mercy, sir!" she cried, "and asking your pardon for troubling you, but I'm feared o' the young leddy, sir; she is not in her room."

"Why, there she is," said I, standing up and glancing through the casement. "She has gone back for the flowers she left upon the bank."

"Oh, sir, see her boots and her dress!" cried the landlady, wildly. "I wish her mother was here, sir — I do. Where she has been is more than I ken, but her bed has not been lain on this night."

"She has felt restless, doubtless, and went for a walk, though the hour was certainly a strange one."

Mrs. Adams pursed her lip and shook her head. But then as she stood at the casement, the girl beneath looked smilingly up at her and beckoned to her with a merry gesture to open the window.

"Have you my tea there?" she asked in a rich, clear voice, with a touch of the mincing French accent.

"It is in your room, miss."

"Look at my boots, Mrs. Adams!" she cried, thrusting them out from under her skirt. "These fells of yours are dreadful places — effroyable — one inch, two inch; never have I seen such mud! My dress, too — *voilà*!"

"Eh, miss, but you are in a pickle," cried the landlady, as she gazed down at the bedraggled gown. "But you must be main weary and heavy for sleep."

"No, no," she answered, laughingly, "I care not for sleep. What is sleep? it is a little death — *voilà tout*. But for me to walk, to run, to beathe the air — that is to live. I was not tired, and so all night I have explored these fells of Yorkshire."

"Lord 'a mercy, miss, and where did you go?" asked Mrs. Adams.

She waved her hand round in a sweeping gesture which included the whole western horizon. "There," she cried. "O comme elles sont tristes et sauvages, ces collines! But I have flowers here. You will give me water, will you not? They will wither else." She gathered her treasures in her lap, and a moment later we heard her light, springy footfall upon the stair.

So she had been out all night, this strange

woman. What motive could have taken her from her snug room on to the bleak, wind-swept hills? Could it be merely the restlessness, the love of adventure of a young girl? Or was there, possibly, some deeper meaning in this nocturnal journey?

Deep as were the mysteries which my studies had taught me to solve, here was a human problem which for the moment at least was beyond my comprehension. I had walked out on the moor in the forenoon, and on my return, as I topped the brow that overlooks the little town, I saw my fellow-lodger some little distance off among the gorse. She had raised a light easel in front of her, and with papered board laid across it, was preparing to paint the magnificent landscape of rock and moor which stretched away in front of her. As I watched her I saw that she was looking anxiously to right and left. Close by me a pool of water had formed in a hollow. Dipping the cup of my pocket-flask into it, I carried it across to her.

"Miss Cameron, I believe," said I. "I am your fellow-lodger. Upperton is my name. We must introduce ourselves in these wilds if we are not to be for ever strangers."

"Oh, then, you live also with Mrs. Adams!" she cried. "I had thought that there were none but peasants in this strange place."

"I am a visitor, like yourself," I answered. "I am a student, and have come for quiet and repose, which my studies demand."

"Quiet, indeed!" said she, glancing round at the

vast circle of silent moors, with the one tiny line of grey cottages which sloped down beneath us.

"And yet not quiet enough," I answered, laughing, "for I have been forced to move further into the fells for the absolute peace which I require."

"Have you, then, built a house upon the fells?" she asked, arching her eyebrows.

"I have, and hope within a few days to occupy it."

"Ah, but that is *triste*," she cried. "And where is it, then, this house which you have built?"

"It is over yonder," I answered. "See that stream which lies like a silver band upon the distant moor? It is the Gaster Beck, and it runs through Gaster Fell."

She started, and turned upon me her great dark, questioning eyes with a look in which surprise, incredulity, and something akin to horror seemed to be struggling for mastery.

"And you will live on the Gaster Fell?" she cried.

"So I have planned. But what do you know of Gaster Fell, Miss Cameron?" I asked. "I had thought that you were a stranger in these parts."

"Indeed, I have never been here before," she answered. "But I have heard my brother talk of these Yorkshire moors; and, if I mistake not, I have heard him name this very one as the wildest and most savage of them all."

"Very likely," said I, carelessly. "It is indeed a dreary place."

"Then why live there?" she cried, eagerly. "Consider the loneliness, the barrenness, the want of all comfort and of all aid, should aid be needed."

"Aid! What aid should be needed on Gaster Fell?"

She looked down and shrugged her shoulders. "Sickness may come in all places," said she. "If I were a man I do not think I would live alone on Gaster Fell."

"I have braved worse dangers than that," said I, laughing; "but I fear that your picture will be spoiled, for the clouds are banking up, and already I feel a few raindrops."

Indeed, it was high time we were on our way to shelter, for even as I spoke there came the sudden, steady swish of the shower. Laughing merrily, my companion threw her light shawl over her head, and, seizing picture and easel, ran with the lithe grace of a young fawn down the furze-clad slope, while I followed after with camp-stool and paint-box.

* * * * *

It was the eve of my departure from Kirkby-Malhouse that we sat upon the green bank in the garden, she with dark dreamy eyes looking sadly out over the sombre fells; while I, with a book upon my knee, glanced covertly at her lovely profile and marvelled to myself how twenty years of life could have stamped so sad and wistful an expression upon it.

"You have read much," I remarked at last. "Women have opportunities now such as their mothers never knew. Have you ever thought of going further — or seeking a course of college or even a learned profession?"

She smiled wearily at the thought.

"I have no aim, no ambition," she said. "My future is black — confused — a chaos. My life is like to one of these paths upon the fells. You have seen them, Monsieur Upperton. They are smooth and straight and clear where they begin; but soon they wind to left and wind to right, and so mid rocks and crags until they lose themselves in some quagmire. At Brussels my path was straight; but now, *mon Dieu*! who is there can tell me where it leads?"

"It might take no prophet to do that, Miss Cameron," quoth I, with the fatherly manner which two-score years may show toward one. "If I may read your life, I would venture to say that you were destined to fulfil the lot of women — to make some good man happy, and to shed around, in some wider circle, the pleasure which your society has given me since first I knew you."

"I will never marry," said she, with a sharp decision, which surprised and somewhat amused me.

"Not marry — and why?"

A strange look passed over her sensitive features, and she plucked nervously at the grass on the bank beside her.

"I dare not," said she in a voice that quivered with emotion.

"Dare not?"

"It is not for me. I have other things to do. That path of which I spoke is one which I must tread alone."

"But this is morbid," said I. "Why should your lot, Miss Cameron, be separate from that of my own sisters, or the thousand other young ladies whom every season brings out into the world? But perhaps it is that you have a fear and distrust of mankind. Marriage brings a risk as well as a happiness."

"The risk would be with the man who married me," she cried. And then in an instant, as though she had said too much, she sprang to her feet and drew her mantle round her. "The night air is chill, Mr. Upperton," said she, and so swept swiftly away, leaving me to muse over the strange words which had fallen from her lips.

Clearly, it was time that I should go. I set my teeth and vowed that another day should not have passed before I should have snapped this newly formed tie and sought the lonely retreat which awaited me upon the moors. Breakfast was hardly over in the morning before a peasant dragged up to the door the rude hand-cart which was to convey my few personal belongings to my new dwelling. My fellow-lodger had kept her room; and, steeled as my mind was against her influence, I was yet conscious of a little throb of disappointment that she should allow me to depart without a word of farewell. My hand-cart with its load of books had already started, and I, having shaken hands with Mrs. Adams, was about to follow it, when there was a quick scurry of feet on the stair, and there she was beside me all panting with her own haste.

"Then you go — you really go?" said she.

"My studies call me."

"And to Gaster Fell?" she asked.

"Yes; to the cottage which I have built there."

"And you will live alone there?"

"With my hundred companions who lie in that cart."

"Ah, books!" she cried, with a pretty shrug of her graceful shoulders. "But you will make me a promise?"

"What is it?" I asked, in surprise.

"It is a small thing. You will not refuse me?"

"You have but to ask it."

She bent forward her beautiful face with an expression of the most intense earnestness. "You will bolt your door at night?" said she; and was gone ere I could say a word in answer to her extraordinary request.

It was a strange thing for me to find myself at last duly installed in my lonely dwelling. For me, now, the horizon was bounded by the barren circle of wiry, unprofitable grass, patched over with furze bushes and scarred by the profusion of Nature's gaunt and granite ribs. A duller, wearier waste I have never seen; but its dullness was its very charm.

And yet the very first night which I spent at Gaster Fell there came a strange incident to lead my thoughts back once more to the world which I had left behind me.

It had been a sullen and sultry evening, with great livid cloud-banks mustering in the west. As the night wore on, the air within my little cabin became closer and more oppressive. A weight seemed to rest upon my brow and my chest. From far away the low rumble of thunder came moaning over the moor. Unable to sleep, I dressed, and standing at my cottage door, looked on the black solitude which surrounded me.

Taking the narrow sheep path which ran by this stream, I strolled along it for some hundred yards, and had turned to retrace my steps, when the moon was finally buried beneath an ink-black cloud, and the darkness deepened so suddenly that I could see neither the path at my feet, the stream upon my right, nor the rocks upon my left. I was standing groping about in the thick gloom, when there came a crash of thunder with a flash of lightning which lighted up the whole vast fell, so that every bush and rock stood out clear and hard in the vivid light. It was but for an instant, and yet that momentary view struck a thrill of fear and astonishment through me, for in my very path, not twenty yards before me, there stood a woman, the livid light beating upon her face and showing up every detail of her dress and features.

There was no mistaking those dark eyes, that tall, graceful figure. It was she — Eva Cameron, the woman whom I thought I had for ever left. For an instant I stood petrified, marvelling whether this could indeed be she, or whether it was some figment conjured up by my excited brain. Then I ran swiftly forward in the direction where I had seen her, calling loudly upon her, but without reply. Again I called, and again no answer came back, save the melancholy wail of the owl. A second flash illuminated the landscape, and the moon burst out from behind its cloud. But I could not, though I climbed upon a knoll which overlooked the whole moor, see any sign of this strange midnight wanderer. For an hour or more I traversed the fell, and at last found myself back at my little cabin, still uncertain as to whether it had been a woman or a shadow upon which I gazed.

III — OF THE GREY COTTAGE IN THE GLEN

It was either on the fourth or the fifth day after I had taken possession of my cottage that I was astonished to hear footsteps upon the grass outside, quickly followed by a crack, as from a stick upon the door. The explosion of an infernal machine would hardly have surprised or discomfited me more. I had hoped to have shaken off all intrusion for ever, yet here was somebody beating at my door with as little ceremony as if it had been a village ale-house. Hot with anger, I flung down my book and withdrew the bolt just as my visitor had raised his stick to renew his rough application for admittance. He was a tall, powerful man, tawny-bearded and deep-chested, clad in a loose-fitting suit of tweed, cut for comfort rather than elegance. As he stood in the shimmering sunlight, I took in every feature of his face. The large, fleshy nose; the steady blue eyes, with their thick thatch of overhanging brows; the broad forehead, all knitted and lined with furrows, which were strangely at variance with his youthful bearing. In spite of his weather-stained felt hat, and the coloured handkerchief slung round his muscular brown neck, I could see at a glance he was a man of breeding and education. I had been prepared for some wandering shepherd or uncouth tramp, but this apparition fairly disconcerted me.

"You look astonished," said he, with a smile. "Did you think, then, that you were the only man in the world with a taste for solitude? You see that there are other hermits in the wilderness besides yourself."

"Do you mean to say that you live here?" I asked in no conciliatory voice.

"Up yonder," he answered, tossing his head backward. "I thought as we were neighbours, Mr. Upperton, that I could not do less than look in and see if I could assist you in any way."

"Thank you," I said coldly, standing with my hand upon the latch of the door. "I am a man of simple tastes, and you can do nothing for me. You have the advantage of me in knowing my name."

He appeared to be chilled by my ungracious manner.

"I learned it from the masons who were at work here," he said. "As for me, I am a surgeon, the surgeon of Gaster Fell. That is the name I have gone by in these parts, and it serves as well as another."

"Not much room for practice here?" I observed.

"Not a soul except yourself for miles on either side."

"You appear to have had need of some assistance yourself," I remarked, glancing at a broad white splash, as from the recent action of some powerful acid, upon his sunburnt cheek.

"That is nothing," he answered, curtly, turning his face half round to hide the mark. "I must get back, for I have a companion who is waiting for me. If I can ever do anything for you, pray let me know. You have only to follow the beck upward for a mile or so to find my place. Have you a bolt on the inside of your door?"

"Yes," I answered, rather startled at this question.

"Keep it bolted, then," he said. "The fell is a strange place. You never know who may be about. It is as well to be on the safe side. Goodbye." He raised his hat, turned on his heel and lounged away along the bank of the little stream.

I was still standing with my hand upon the latch, gazing after my unexpected visitor, when I became aware of yet another dweller in the wilderness. Some distance along the path which the stranger was taking there lay a great grey boulder, and leaning against this was a small, wizened man, who stood erect as the other approached, and advanced to meet him. The two talked for a minute or more, the taller man nodding his head frequently in my direction, as though describing what had passed between us. Then they walked on together, and disappeared in a dip of the fell. Presently I saw them ascending once more some rising ground farther on. My acquaintance had thrown his arm round his elderly friend, either from affection or from a desire to aid him up the steep incline. The square burly figure and its shrivelled, meagre companion stood out against the sky-line, and turning their faces, they looked back at me. At the sight, I slammed the door, lest they should be encouraged to return. But when I peeped from the window some minutes afterward, I perceived that they were gone.

All day I bent over the Egyptian papyrus upon which I was engaged; but neither the subtle reasonings of the ancient philosopher of Memphis, nor the mystic meaning which lay in his pages, could raise my mind from the things of earth. Evening was drawing in before I threw my work aside in despair. My heart was bitter against this man for his intrusion. Standing by the beck which purled past the door of my cabin, I cooled my heated brow, and thought the matter over. Clearly it was the small mystery hanging over these neighbours of mine which had caused my mind to run so persistently on them. That cleared up, they would no longer cause an obstacle to my studies. What was to hinder me, then, from walking in the direction of their dwelling, and observing for myself, without permitting them to suspect my presence, what manner of men they might be? Doubtless, their mode of life would be found to admit of some simple and prosaic explanation. In any case, the evening was fine, and a walk would be bracing for mind and body. Lighting my pipe, I set off over the moors in the direction which they had taken.

About half-way down a wild glen there stood a small clump of gnarled and stunted oak trees. From behind these, a thin dark column of smoke rose into the still evening air. Clearly this marked the position of my neighbour's house. Trending away to the left, I was able to gain the shelter of a line of rocks, and so reach a spot from which I could command a view of the building without exposing myself to any risk of being observed. It was a small, slate-covered cottage, hardly larger than the boulders among which it lay. Like my own cabin, it showed signs of having been constructed for the use of some shepherd; but, unlike mine, no pains had been taken by the tenants to improve and enlarge it. Two little peeping windows, a cracked and weather-beaten door, and a discoloured barrel for catching the rain water, were the only external objects from which I might draw deductions as to the dwellers within. Yet even in these there was food for thought, for as I drew nearer, still concealing myself behind the ridge, I saw that thick bars of iron covered the windows, while the old door was slashed and plated with the same metal. These strange precautions, together with the wild surroundings and unbroken solitude, gave an indescribably ill omen and fearsome character to the solitary building. Thrusting my pipe into my pocket, I crawled upon my hands and knees through the gorse and ferns until I was within a hundred yards of my neighbour's door. There, finding that I could not approach nearer without fear of detection, I crouched down, and set myself to watch.

I had hardly settled into my hiding place, when the door of the cottage swung open, and the man who had introduced himself to me as the surgeon of Gaster Fell came out, bareheaded, with a spade in his hands. In front of the door there was a small cultivated patch containing potatoes, peas and other forms of green stuff, and here he proceeded to busy himself, trimming, weeding and arranging, singing the while in a powerful though not very musical voice. He was all engrossed in his work, with his back to the cottage, when there emerged from the half-open door the same attenuated creature whom I had seen in the morning. I could perceive now that he was a man of sixty, wrinkled, bent, and feeble, with sparse, grizzled hair, and long, colourless face. With a cringing, sidelong gait, he shuffled toward his companion, who was unconscious of his approach until he was close upon him. His light footfall or his breathing may have finally given notice of his proximity, for the worker sprang round and faced him. Each made a quick step toward the other, as though in greeting, and then — even now I feel the horror of the instant — the tall man rushed upon and knocked his companion to the earth, then whipping up his body, ran with great speed over the intervening ground and disappeared with his burden into the house.

Case hardened as I was by my varied life, the suddenness and violence of the thing made me shudder. The man's age, his feeble frame, his humble and deprecating manner, all cried shame against the deed. So hot was my anger, that I was on the point of striding up to the cabin, unarmed as I was, when the sound of voices from within showed me that the victim had recovered. The sun had sunk beneath the horizon, and all was grey, save a red feather in the cap of Pennigent. Secure in the failing light, I approached near and strained my ears to catch what was passing. I could hear the high, querulous voice of the elder man and the deep, rough monotone of his assailant, mixed with a strange metallic jangling and clanking. Presently the surgeon came out, locked the door behind him and stamped up and down in the twilight, pulling at his hair and brandishing his arms, like a man demented. Then he set off, walking rapidly up the valley, and I soon lost sight of him among the rocks.

When his footsteps had died away in the distance, I drew nearer to the cottage. The prisoner within was still pouring forth a stream of words, and moaning from time to time like a man in pain. These words resolved themselves, as I approached, into prayers — shrill, voluble prayers, pattered forth with the intense earnestness of one who sees impending an imminent danger. There was to me something inexpressibly awesome in this gush of solemn entreaty from the lonely sufferer, meant for no human ear, and jarring upon the silence of the night. I was still pondering whether I should mix myself in the affair or not, when I heard in the distance the sound of the surgeon's returning footfall. At that I drew myself up quickly by the iron bars and glanced in through the diamond-paned window. The interior of the cottage was lighted up by a lurid glow, coming from what I afterward discovered to be a chemical furnace. By its rich light I could distinguish a great litter of retorts, test tubes and condensers, which sparkled over the table, and threw strange, grotesque shadows on the wall. On the further side of the room was a wooden framework resembling a hencoop, and in this, still absorbed in prayer, knelt the man whose voice I heard. The red glow beating upon his upturned face made it stand out from the shadow like a painting from Rembrandt, showing up every wrinkle upon the parchment-like skin. I had but time for a fleeting glance; then, dropping from the window, I made off through the rocks and the heather, nor slackened my pace until I found myself back in my cabin once more. There I threw myself upon my couch, more disturbed and shaken than I had ever thought to feel again.

Such doubts as I might have had as to whether I had indeed seen my former fellow-lodger upon the night of the thunderstorm were resolved the next morning. Strolling along down the path which led to the fell, I saw in one spot where the ground was soft the impressions of a foot — the small, dainty foot of a well-booted woman. That tiny heel and high instep could have belonged to none other than my companion of Kirkby-Malhouse. I followed her trail for some distance, till it still pointed, as far as I could discern it, to the lonely and ill-omened cottage. What power could there be to draw this tender girl, through wind and rain and darkness, across the fearsome moors to that strange rendezvous?

I have said that a little beck flowed down the

valley and past my very door. A week or so after the doings which I have described, I was seated by my window when I perceived something white drifting slowly down the stream. My first thought was that it was a drowning sheep; but picking up my stick, I strolled to the bank and hooked it ashore. On examination it proved to be a large sheet, torn and tattered, with the initials J. C. in the corner. What gave it its sinister significance, however, was that from hem to hem it was all dabbled and discoloured.

Shutting the door of my cabin, I set off up the glen in the direction of the surgeon's cabin. I had not gone far before I perceived the very man himself. He was walking rapidly along the hillside, beating the furze bushes with a cudgel and bellowing like a madman. Indeed, at the sight of him, the doubts as to his sanity which had arisen in my mind were strengthened and confirmed.

As he approached I noticed that his left arm was suspended in a sling. On perceiving me he stood irresolute, as though uncertain whether to come over to me or not. I had no desire for an interview with him, however, so I hurried past him, on which he continued on his way, still shouting and striking about with his club. When he had disappeared over the fells, I made my way down to his cottage, determined to find some clue to what had occurred. I was surprised, on reaching it, to find the iron-plated door flung wide open. The ground immediately outside it was marked with the signs of a struggle. The chemical apparatus within and the furniture were all dashed about and shattered. Most suggestive of all, the sinister wooden cage was stained with bloodmarks, and its unfortunate occupant had disappeared. My heart was heavy for the little man, for I was assured I should never see him in this world more.

There was nothing in the cabin to throw any light upon the identity of my neighbours. The room was stuffed with chemical instruments. In one corner a small bookcase contained a choice selection of works of science. In another was a pile of geological specimens collected from the limestone.

I caught no glimpse of the surgeon upon my homeward journey; but when I reached my cottage I was astonished and indignant to find that somebody had entered it in my absence. Boxes had been pulled out from under the bed, the curtains disarranged, the chairs drawn out from the wall. Even my study had not been safe from this rough intruder, for the prints of a heavy boot were plainly visible on the ebony-black carpet.

IV — OF THE MAN WHO CAME IN THE NIGHT

The night set in gusty and tempestuous, and the moon was all girt with ragged clouds. The wind blew in melancholy gusts, sobbing and sighing over the moor, and setting all the gorse bushes agroaning. From time to time a little sputter of rain pattered up against the window-pane. I sat until near midnight, glancing over the fragment on immortality by Iamblichus, the Alexandrian platonist, of whom the Emperor Julian said that he was posterior to Plato in time but not in genius. At last, shutting up my book, I opened my door and took a last look at the dreary fell and still more dreary sky. As I protruded my head, a swoop of wind caught me and sent the red ashes of my pipe sparkling and dancing through the darkness. At the same moment the moon shone brilliantly out from between two clouds, and I saw, sitting on the hillside, not two hundred yards from my door, the man who called himself the surgeon of Gaster Fell. He was squatted among the heather, his elbows upon his knees, and his chin resting upon his hands, as motionless as a stone, with his gaze fixed steadily upon the door of my dwelling.

At the sight of this ill-omened sentinel, a chill of horror and of fear shot through me, for his gloomy and mysterious associations had cast a glamour round the man, and the hour and place were in keeping with his sinister presence. In a moment, however, a manly glow of resentment and self-confidence drove this petty emotion from my mind, and I strode fearlessly in his direction. He rose as I approached and faced me, with the moon shining on his grave, bearded face and glittering on his eyeballs. "What is the meaning of this?" I cried, as I came upon him. "What right have you to play the spy on me?"

I could see the flush of anger rise on his face. "Your stay in the country has made you forget your manners," he said. "The moor is free to all."

"You will say next that my house is free to all," I said, hotly. "You have had the impertience to ransack it in my absence this afternoon."

He started, and his features showed the most intense excitement. "I swear to you that I had no hand in it!" he cried. "I have never set foot in your house in my life. Oh, sir, sir, if you will but believe me, there is a danger hanging over you, and you would do well to be careful."

"I have had enough of you," I said. "I saw that cowardly blow you struck when you thought no human eye rested upon you. I have been to your cottage, too, and know all that it has to tell. If there is a law in England, you shall hang for what you have done. As to me, I am an old soldier, sir, and I am armed. I shall not fasten my door. But if you or any other villain attempt to cross my threshold it shall be at your own risk." With these words, I swung round upon my heel and strode into my cabin.

For two days the wind freshened and increased, with constant squalls of rain until on the third night the most furious storm was raging which I can ever recollect in England. I felt that it was positively useless to go to bed, nor could I concentrate my mind sufficiently to read a book. I turned my lamp half down to moderate the glare, and leaning back in my chair, I gave myself up to reverie. I must have lost all perception of time, for I have no recollection how long I sat there on the borderland betwixt thought and slumber. At last, about 3 or possibly 4 o'clock, I came to myself with a start — not only came to myself, but with every sense and nerve upon the strain. Looking round my chamber in the dim light, I could not see anything to justify my sudden trepidation. The homely room, the rain-blurred window and the rude wooden door were all as they had been. I had begun to persuade myself that some half-formed dream had sent that vague thrill through my nerves, when in a moment I became conscious of what it was. It was a sound — the sound of a human step outside my solitary cottage.

Amid the thunder and the rain and the wind I could hear it — a dull, stealthy footfall, now on the grass, now on the stones — occasionally stopping entirely, then resumed, and ever drawing nearer. I sat breathlessly, listening to the eerie sound. It had stopped now at my very door, and was replaced by a panting and gasping, as of one who has travelled fast and far.

By the flickering light of the expiring lamp I could see that the latch of my door was twitching, as though a gentle pressure was exerted on it from without. Slowly, slowly, it rose, until it was free of the catch, and then there was a pause of a quarter minute or more, while I still eat silent with dilated eyes and drawn sabre. Then, very slowly, the door began to revolve upon its hinges, and the keen air of the night came whistling through the slit. Very cautiously it was pushed open, so that never a sound came from the rusty hinges. As the aperture enlarged, I became aware of a dark, shadowy figure upon my threshold, and of a pale face that looked in at me. The features were human, but the eyes were not. They seemed to burn through the darkness with a greenish brilliancy of their own; and in their baleful, shifty glare I was conscious of the very spirit of murder. Springing from my chair, I had raised my naked sword, when, with a wild shouting, a second figure dashed up to my door. At its approach my shadowy visitant uttered a shrill cry, and fled away across the fells, yelping like a beaten hound.

Tingling with my recent fear, I stood at my door, peering through the night with the discordant cry of the fugitives still ringing in my ears. At that moment a vivid flash of lightning illuminated the whole landscape and made it as clear as day. By its light I saw far away upon the hillside two dark figures pursuing each other with extreme rapidity across the fells. Even at that distance the contrast between them forbid all doubt as to their identity. The first was the small, elderly man, whom I had supposed to be dead; the second was my neighbour, the surgeon. For an instant they stood out clear and hard in the unearthly light; in the next, the darkness had closed over them, and they were gone. As I turned to re-enter my chamber, my foot rattled against something on my threshold. Stooping, I found it was a straight knife, fashioned entirely of lead, and so soft and brittle that it was a strange choice for a weapon. To render it more harmless, the top had been cut square off. The edge, however, had been assiduously sharpened against a stone, as was evident from the markings upon it, so that it was still a dangerous implement in the grasp of a determined man.

And what was the meaning of it all? you ask. Many a drama which I have come across in my wandering life, some as strange and as striking as this one, has lacked the ultimate explanation which you demand. Fate is a grand weaver of tales; but she ends them, as a rule, in defiance of all artistic laws, and with an unbecoming want of regard for literary propriety. As it happens, however, I have a letter before me as I write which I may add without comment, and which will clear all that may remain dark.

"Kirkby Lunatic Asylum,
"*September 4th*, 1885.

"Sir, — I am deeply conscious that some apology and explanation is due to you for the very startling and, in your eyes, mysterious events which have recently occurred, and which have so seriously interfered with the retired existence which you desire to lead. I should have called upon you on the morning after the recapture of my father, but my knowledge of your dislike to visitors and also of — you will excuse my saying it — your very violent temper, led me to think that it was better to communicate with you by letter.

"My poor father was a hard-working general practitioner in Birmingham, where his name is still remembered and respected. About ten years ago he began to show signs of mental aberration, which we were inclined to put down to overwork and the effects of a sunstroke. Feeling my own incompetence to pronounce upon a case of such importance, I at once sought the highest advice in Birmingham and London. Among others we consulted the eminent alienist, Mr. Fraser Brown, who pronounced my father's case to be intermittent in its nature, but dangerous during the paroxysms. 'It may take a homicidal, or it may take a religious turn,' he said; 'or it may prove to be a mixture of both. For months he may be as well as you or me, and then in a moment he may break out. You will incur a great responsibility if you leave him without supervision.'

"I need say no more, sir. You will understand

the terrible task which has fallen upon my poor sister and me in endeavouring to save my father from the asylum which in his sane moments filled him with horror. I can only regret that your peace has been disturbed by our misfortunes, and I offer you in my sister's name and my own our apologies."

"Yours truly,
"J. Cameron."

VIII. HOW IT HAPPENED

She was a writing medium. This is what she wrote: —

I can remember some things upon that evening most distinctly, and others are like some vague, broken dreams. That is what makes it so difficult to tell a connected story. I have no idea now what it was that had taken me to London and brought me back so late. It just merges into all my other visits to London. But from the time that I got out at the little country station everything is extraordinarily clear. I can live it again — every instant of it.

I remember so well walking down the platform and looking at the illuminated clock at the end which told me that it was half-past eleven. I remember also my wondering whether I could get home before midnight. Then I remember the big motor, with its glaring head-lights and glitter of polished brass, waiting for me outside. It was my new thirty-horse-power Robur, which had only been delivered that day. I remember also asking Perkins, my chauffeur, how she had gone, and his saying that he thought she was excellent.

"I'll try her myself," said I, and I climbed into the driver's seat.

"The gears are not the same," said he. "Perhaps, sir, I had better drive."

"No; I should like to try her," said I.

And so we started on the five-mile drive for home.

My old car had the gears as they used always to be in notches on a bar. In this car you passed the gear-lever through a gate to get on the higher ones. It was not difficult to master, and soon I thought that I understood it. It was foolish, no doubt, to begin to learn a new system in the dark, but one often does foolish things, and one has not always to pay the full price for them. I got along very well until I came to Claystall Hill. It is one of the worst hills in England, a mile and a half long and one in six in places, with three fairly sharp curves. My park gates stand at the very foot of it upon the main London road.

We were just over the brow of this hill, where the grade is steepest, when the trouble began. I had been on the top speed, and wanted to get her on the free; but she stuck between gears, and I had to get her back on the top again. By this time she was going at a great rate, so I clapped on both brakes, and one after the other they gave way. I didn't mind so much when I felt my footbrake snap, but when I put all my weight on my side-brake, and the lever clanged to its full limit without a catch, it brought a cold sweat out of me. By this time we were fairly tearing down the slope. The lights were brilliant, and I brought her round the first curve all right. Then we did the second one, though it was a close shave for the ditch. There was a mile of straight then with the third curve beneath it, and after that the gate of the park. If I could shoot into that harbour all would be well, for the slope up to the house would bring her to a stand.

Perkins behaved splendidly. I should like that to be known. He was perfectly cool and alert. I had thought at the very beginning of taking the bank, and he read my intention.

"I wouldn't do it, sir," said he. "At this pace it must go over and we should have it on the top of us."

Of course he was right. He got to the electric switch and had it off, so we were in the free; but we were still running at a fearful pace. He laid his hands on the wheel.

"I'll keep her steady," said he, "if you care to jump and chance it. We can never get round that curve. Better jump, sir."

"No," said I; "I'll stick it out. You can jump if you like."

"I'll stick it with you, sir," said he.

If it had been the old car I should have jammed the gear-lever into the reverse, and seen what would happen. I expect she would have stripped her gears or smashed up somehow, but it would have been a chance. As it was, I was helpless. Perkins tried to climb across, but you couldn't do it going at that pace. The wheels were whirring like a high wind and the big body creaking and groaning with the strain. But the lights were brilliant, and one could steer to an inch. I remember thinking what an awful and yet majestic sight we should appear to any one who met us. It was a narrow road, and we were just a great, roaring, golden death to any one who came in our path.

We got round the corner with one wheel three

feet high upon the bank. I thought we were surely over, but after staggering for a moment she righted and darted onwards. That was the third corner and the last one. There was only the park gate now. It was facing us, but, as luck would have it, not facing us directly. It was about twenty yards to the left up the main road into which we ran. Perhaps I could have done it, but I expect that the steering-gear had been jarred when we ran on the bank. The wheel did not turn easily. We shot out of the lane. I saw the open gate on the left. I whirled round my wheel with all the strength of my wrists. Perkins and I threw our bodies across, and then the next instant, going at fifty miles an hour, my right front wheel struck full on the right-hand pillar of my own gate. I heard the crash. I was conscious of flying through the air, and then − and then − !

* * * * *

When I became aware of my own existence once more I was among some brushwood in the shadow of the oaks upon the lodge side of the drive. A man was standing beside me. I imagined at first that it was Perkins, but when I looked again I saw that it was Stanley, a man whom I had known at college some years before, and for whom I had a really genuine affection. There was always something peculiarly sympathetic to me in Stanley's personality; and I was proud to think that I had some similar influence upon him. At the present moment I was surprised to see him, but I was like a man in a dream, giddy and shaken and quite prepared to take things as I found them without questioning them.

"What a smash!" I said. "Good Lord, what an awful smash!"

He nodded his head, and even in the gloom I could see that he was smiling the gentle, wistful smile which I connected with him.

I was quite unable to move. Indeed, I had not any desire to try to move. But my senses were exceedingly alert. I saw the wreck of the motor lit up by the moving lanterns. I saw the little group of people and heard the hushed voices. There were the lodge-keeper and his wife, and one or two more. They were taking no notice of me, but were very busy round the car. Then suddenly I heard a cry of pain.

"The weight is on him. Lift it easy," cried a voice.

"It's only my leg!" said another one, which I recognized as Perkins's. "Where's master?" he cried.

"Here I am," I answered, but they did not seem to hear me. They were all bending over something which lay in front of the car.

Stanley laid his hand upon my shoulder, and his touch was inexpressibly soothing. I felt light and happy, in spite of all.

"No pain, of course?" said he.

"None," said I.

"There never is," said he.

And then suddenly a wave of amazement passed over me. Stanley! Stanley! Why, Stanley had surely died of enteric at Bloemfontein in the Boer War!

"Stanley!" I cried, and the words seemed to choke my throat — "Stanley, you are dead."

He looked at me with the same old gentle, wistful smile.

"So are you," he answered.

IX. THE PRISONER'S DEFENCE

The circumstances, so far as they were known to the public, concerning the death of the beautiful Miss Ena Garnier, and the fact that Captain John Fowler, the accused officer, had refused to defend himself on the occasion of the proceedings at the police-court, had roused very general interest. This was increased by the statement that, though he withheld his defence, it would be found to be of a very novel and convincing character. The assertion of the prisoner's lawyer at the police-court, to the effect that the answer to the charge was such that it could not yet be given, but would be available before the Assizes, also caused much speculation. A final touch was given to the curiosity of the public when it was learned that the prisoner had refused all offers of legal assistance from counsel and was determined to conduct his own defence. The case for the Crown was ably presented, and was generally considered to be a very damning one, since it showed very clearly that the accused was subject to fits of jealousy, and that he had already been guilty of some violence owing to this cause. The prisoner listened to the evidence without emotion, and neither interrupted nor cross-questioned the witnesses. Finally, on being informed that the time had come when he might address the jury, he stepped to the front of the dock. He was a man of striking appearance, swarthy, black-moustached, nervous, and virile, with a quietly confident manner. Taking a paper from his pocket he read the following statement, which made the deepest impression upon the crowded court: —

I would wish to say, in the first place, gentlemen of the jury, that, owing to the generosity of my brother officers — for my own means are limited — I might have been defended to-day by the first talent of the Bar. The reason I have declined their assistance and have determined to fight my own case is not that I have any confidence in my own abilities or eloquence, but it is because I am convinced that a plain, straightforward tale, coming direct from the man who has been the tragic actor in this dreadful affair, will impress you more than any indirect statement could do. If I had felt that I were guilty I should have asked for help. Since, in my own heart, I believe that I am innocent, I am pleading my own cause, feeling that my plain words of truth and reason will have more weight with you than the most learned and eloquent advocate. By the indulgence of the Court I have been permitted to put my remarks upon paper, so that I may reproduce certain conversations and be assured of saying neither more nor less than I mean.

It will be remembered that at the trial at the police-court two months ago I refused to defend myself. This has been referred to to-day as a proof of my guilt. I said that it would be some days before I could open my mouth. This was taken at the time as a subterfuge. Well, the days are over, and I am now able to make clear to you not only what took place, but also why it was impossible for me to give any explanation. I will tell you now exactly what I did and why it was that I did it. If you, my fellow-countrymen, think that I did wrong, I will make no complaint, but will suffer in silence any penalty which you may impose upon me.

I am a soldier of fifteen years' standing, a captain in the Second Breconshire Battalion. I have served in the South African Campaign and was mentioned in despatches after the battle of Diamond Hill. When the war broke out with Germany I was seconded from my regiment, and I was appointed as adjutant to the First Scottish Scouts, newly raised. The regiment was quartered at Radchurch, in Essex, where the men were placed partly in huts and were partly billeted upon the inhabitants. All the officers were billeted out, and my quarters were with Mr. Murreyfield, the local squire. It was there that I first met Miss Ena Garnier.

It may not seem proper at such a time and place as this that I should describe that lady. And yet her personality is the very essence of my case. Let me only say that I cannot believe that Nature ever put into female form a more exquisite combination of beauty and intelligence. She was twenty-five years of age, blonde and tall, with a peculiar delicacy of features and of expression. I have read of people falling in love at first sight, and had always looked upon it as an expression of the novelist. And yet from the moment that I saw Ena Garnier life held for me but the one ambition — that she should be mine. I had never dreamed before of the possibilities of passion that were within me. I will not enlarge upon the subject, but to make you understand my action — for I wish you to comprehend it, however much you may condemn it — you must realize that I was in the grip of a frantic elementary passion which made, for a time, the world and all that was in it seem a small thing if I could but gain the love of this one girl. And yet, in justice to myself, I will say that there was always one thing which I placed above her. That was my honour as a soldier and a gentleman. You will find it hard to believe this when I tell you what occurred, and yet — though for one moment I forgot myself — my whole legal offence consists in my desperate endeavour to retrieve what I had done.

I soon found that the lady was not insensible to the advances which I made to her. Her position in the household was a curious one. She had come a year before from Montpellier, in the South of France, in answer to an advertisement from the Murreyfields in order to teach French to their three young children. She was, however, unpaid, so that she was rather a friendly guest than an *employée*. She had always, as I gathered, been fond of the English and desirous to live in England, but the outbreak of the war had quickened her feelings into passionate attachment, for the ruling emotion of her soul was her hatred of the Germans. Her grandfather, as she told me, had been killed under very tragic circumstances in the campaign of 1870, and her two brothers were both in the French army. Her voice vibrated with passion when she spoke of the infamies of Belgium, and more than once I have seen her kissing my sword and my revolver because she hoped they would be used upon the enemy. With such feelings in her heart it can be imagined that my wooing was not a difficult one. I should have been glad to marry her at once, but to this she would not consent. Everything was to come after the war, for it was necessary, she said, that I should go to Montpellier and meet her people, so that the French proprieties should be properly observed.

She had one accomplishment which was rare for a lady; she was a skilled motor-cyclist. She had been fond of long, solitary rides, but after our engagement I was occasionally allowed to accompany her. She was a woman, however, of strange moods and fancies, which added in my feelings to the charm of her character. She could be tenderness itself, and she could be aloof and even harsh in her manner. More than once she had refused my company with no reason given, and with a quick, angry flash of her eyes when I asked for one. Then, perhaps, her mood would change and she would make up for this unkindness by some exquisite attention which would in an instant soothe all my ruffled feelings. It was the same in the house. My military duties were so exacting that it was only in the evenings that I could hope to see her, and yet very often she remained in the little study which was used during the day for the children's lessons, and would tell me plainly that she wished to be alone. Then, when she saw that I was hurt by her caprice, she would laugh and apologize so sweetly for her rudeness that I was more her slave than ever.

Mention has been made of my jealous disposition, and it has been asserted at the trial that there were scenes owing to my jealousy, and that once Mrs. Murreyfield had to interfere. I admit that I was jealous. When a man loves with the whole strength of his soul it is impossible, I think, that he should be clear of jealousy. The girl was of a very independent spirit. I found that she knew many officers at

Chelmsford and Colchester. She would disappear for hours together upon her motor-cycle. There were questions about her past life which she would only answer with a smile unless they were closely pressed. Then the smile would become a frown. Is it any wonder that I, with my whole nature vibrating with passionate, whole-hearted love, was often torn by jealousy when I came upon those closed doors of her life which she was so determined not to open? Reason came at times and whispered how foolish it was that I should stake my whole life and soul upon one of whom I really knew nothing. Then came a wave of passion once more and reason was submerged.

I have spoken of the closed doors of her life. I was aware that a young, unmarried Frenchwoman has usually less liberty than her English sister. And yet in the case of this lady it continually came out in her conversation that she had seen and known much of the world. It was the more distressing to me as whenever she had made an observation which pointed to this she would afterwards, as I could plainly see, be annoyed by her own indiscretion, and endeavour to remove the impression by every means in her power. We had several small quarrels on this account, when I asked questions to which I could get no answers, but they have been exaggerated in the address for the prosecution. Too much has been made also of the intervention of Mrs. Murreyfield, though I admit that the quarrel was more serious upon that occasion. It arose from my finding the photograph of a man upon her table, and her evident confusion when I asked her for some particulars about him. The name "H. Vardin" was written underneath — evidently an autograph. I was worried by the fact that this photograph had the frayed appearance of one which has been carried secretly about, as a girl might conceal the picture of her lover in her dress. She absolutely refused to give me any information about him, save to make a statement which I found incredible, that it was a man whom she had never seen in her life. It was then that I forgot myself. I raised my voice and declared that I should know more about her life or that I should break with her, even if my own heart should be broken in the parting. I was not violent, but Mrs. Murreyfield heard me from the passage, and came into the room to remonstrate. She was a kind, motherly person who took a sympathetic interest in our romance, and I remember that on this occasion she reproved me for my jealousy and finally persuaded me that I had been unreasonable, so that we became reconciled once more. Ena was so madly fascinating and I so hopelessly her slave that she could always draw me back, however much prudence and reason warned me to escape from her control. I tried again and again to find out about this man Vardin, but was always met by the same assurance, which she repeated with every kind of solemn oath, that she had never seen the man in her life. Why she should carry about the photograph of a man — a young, somewhat sinister man, for I had observed him closely before she snatched the picture from my hand — was what she either could not, or would not, explain.

Then came the time for my leaving Radchurch. I had been appointed to a junior but very responsible post at the War Office, which, of course, entailed my living in London. Even my week-ends found me engrossed with my work, but at last I had a few days' leave of absence. It is those few days which have ruined my life, which have brought me the most horrible experience that ever a man had to undergo, and have finally placed me here in the dock, pleading as I plead to-day for my life and my honour.

It is nearly five miles from the station to Radchurch. She was there to meet me. It was the first time that we had been reunited since I had put all my heart and my soul upon her. I cannot enlarge upon these matters, gentlemen. You will either be able to sympathize with and understand the emotions which overbalance a man at such a time, or you will not. If you have imagination, you will. If you have not, I can never hope to make you see more than the bare fact. That bare fact, placed in the baldest language, is that during this drive from Radchurch Junction to the village I was led into the greatest indiscretion — the greatest dishonour, if you will — of my life. I told the woman a secret, an enormously important secret, which might affect the fate of the war and the lives of many thousands of men.

It was done before I knew it — before I grasped the way in which her quick brain could place various scattered hints together and weave them into one idea. She was wailing, almost weeping, over the fact that the allied armies were held up by the iron line of the Germans. I explained that it was more correct to say that our iron line was holding them up, since they were the invaders. "But is France, is Belgium, *never* to be rid of them?" she cried. "Are we simply to sit in front of their trenches and be content to let them do what they will with ten provinces of France? Oh, Jack, Jack, for God's sake, say something to bring a little hope to my heart, for sometimes I think that it is breaking! You English are stolid. You can bear these things. But we others, we have more nerve, more soul! It is death to us. Tell me! Do tell me that there is hope! And yet it is foolish of me to ask, for, of course, you are only a subordinate at the War Office, and how should you know what is in the mind of your chiefs?"

"Well, as it happens, I know a good deal," I answered. "Don't fret, for we shall certainly get a move on soon."

"Soon! Next year may seem soon to some people."

"It's not next year."

"Must we wait another month?"

"Not even that."

She squeezed my hand in hers. "Oh, my darling boy, you have brought such joy to my heart! What suspense I shall live in now! I think a week of it would kill me."

"Well, perhaps it won't even be a week."

"And tell me," she went on, in her coaxing voice, "tell me just one thing, Jack. Just one, and I will trouble you no more. Is it our brave French soldiers who advance? Or is it your splendid Tommies?

With whom will the honour lie?"

"With both."

"Glorious!" she cried. "I see it all. The attack will be at the point where the French and British lines join. Together they will rush forward in one glorious advance."

"No," I said. "They will not be together."

"But I understood you to say — of course, women know nothing of such matters, but I understood you to say that it would be a joint advance."

"Well, if the French advanced, we will say, at Verdun, and the British advanced at Ypres, even if they were hundreds of miles apart it would still be a joint advance."

"Ah, I see," she cried, clapping her hands with delight. "They would advance at both ends of the line, so that the Boches would not know which way to send their reserves."

"That is exactly the idea — a real advance at Verdun, and an enormous feint at Ypres."

Then suddenly a chill of doubt seized me. I can remember how I sprang back from her and looked hard into her face. "I've told you too much!" I cried. "Can I trust you? I have been mad to say so much."

She was bitterly hurt by my words. That I should for a moment doubt her was more than she could bear. "I would cut my tongue out, Jack, before I would tell any human being one word of what you have said." So earnest was she that my fears died away. I felt that I could trust her utterly. Before we had reached Radchurch I had put the matter from my mind, and we were lost in our joy of the present and in our plans for the future.

I had a business message to deliver to Colonel Worral, who commanded a small camp at Pedley-Woodrow. I went there and was away for about two hours. When I returned I inquired for Miss Garnier, and was told by the maid that she had gone to her bedroom, and that she had asked the groom to bring her motor-bicycle to the door. It seemed to me strange that she should arrange to go out alone when my visit was such a short one. I had gone into her little study to seek her, and here it was that I waited, for it opened on to the hall passage, and she could not pass without my seeing her.

There was a small table in the window of this room at which she used to write. I had seated myself beside this when my eyes fell upon a name written in her large, bold hand-writing. It was a reversed impression upon the blotting-paper which she had used, but there could be no difficulty in reading it. The name was Hubert Vardin. Apparently it was part of the address of an envelope, for underneath I was able to distinguish the initials S.W., referring to a postal division of London, though the actual name of the street had not been clearly reproduced.

Then I knew for the first time that she was actually corresponding with this man whose vile, voluptuous face I had seen in the photograph with the frayed edges. She had clearly lied to me, too, for was it conceivable that she should correspond with a man whom she had never seen? I don't desire to condone my conduct. Put yourself in my place. Imagine that you had my desperately fervid and jealous nature. You would have done what I did, for you could have done nothing else. A wave of fury passed over me. I laid my hands upon the wooden writing-desk. If it had been an iron safe I should have opened it. As it was, it literally flew to pieces before me. There lay the letter itself, placed under lock and key for safety, while the writer prepared to take it from the house. I had no hesitation or scruple, I tore it open. Dishonourable, you will say, but when a man is frenzied with jealousy he hardly knows what he does. This woman, for whom I was ready to give everything, was either faithful to me or she was not. At any cost I would know which.

A thrill of joy passed through me as my eyes fell upon the first words. I had wronged her. "Cher Monsieur Vardin." So the letter began. It was clearly a business letter, nothing else. I was about to replace it in the envelope with a thousand regrets in my mind for my want of faith when a single word at the bottom of the page caught my eyes, and I started as if I had been stung by an adder. "Verdun" — that was the word. I looked again. "Ypres" was immediately below it. I sat down, horror-stricken, by the broken desk, and I read this letter, a translation of which I have in my hand: —

Murreyfield House, Radchurch.

Dear M. Vardin, — Stringer has told me that he has kept you sufficiently informed as to Chelmsford and Colchester, so I have not troubled to write. They have moved the Midland Territorial Brigade and the heavy guns towards the coast near Cromer, but only for a time. It is for training, not embarkation.

And now for my great news, which I have straight from the War Office itself. Within a week there is to be a very severe attack from Verdun, which is to be supported by a holding attack at Ypres. It is all on a very large scale, and you must send off a special Dutch messenger to Von Starmer by the first boat. I hope to get the exact date and some further particulars from my informant to-night, but meanwhile you must act with energy.

I dare not post this here — you know what village postmasters are, so I am taking it into Colchester, where Stringer will include it with his own report which goes by hand. — Yours faithfully, Sophia Heffner.

I was stunned at first as I read this letter, and then a kind of cold, concentrated rage came over me. So this woman was a German and a spy! I thought of her hypocrisy and her treachery towards me, but, above all, I thought of the danger to the Army and the State. A great defeat, the death of thousands of men, might spring from my misplaced confidence. There was still time, by judgment and energy, to stop this frightful evil. I heard her step upon the stairs outside, and an instant later she had come through the doorway. She started, and her face was bloodless as she saw me seated there with the open letter in my hand.

"How did you get that?" she gasped. "How dared you break my desk and steal my letter?"

I said nothing. I simply sat and looked at her and pondered what I should do. She suddenly sprang forward and tried to snatch the letter. I caught her wrist and pushed her down on to the sofa, where she lay, collapsed. Then I rang the bell, and told the maid that I must see Mr. Murreyfield at once.

He was a genial, elderly man, who had treated this woman with as much kindness as if she were his daughter. He was horrified at what I said. I could not show him the letter on account of the secret that it contained, but I made him understand that it was of desperate importance.

"What are we to do?" he asked. "I never could have imagined anything so dreadful. What would you advise us to do?"

"There is only one thing that we can do," I answered. "This woman must be arrested, and in the meanwhile we must so arrange matters that she cannot possibly communicate with any one. For all we know, she has confederates in this very village. Can you undertake to hold her securely while I go to Colonel Worral at Pedley and get a warrant and a guard?"

"We can lock her in her bedroom."

"You need not trouble," said she. "I give you my word that I will stay where I am. I advise you to be careful, Captain Fowler. You've shown once before that you are liable to do things before you have thought of the consequence. If I am arrested all the world will know that you have given away the secrets that were confided to you. There is an end of your career, my friend. You can punish me, no doubt. What about yourself?"

"I think," said I, "you had best take her to her bedroom."

"Very good, if you wish it," said she, and followed us to the door. When we reached the hall she suddenly broke away, dashed through the entrance, and made for her motor-bicycle, which was standing there. Before she could start we had both seized her. She stooped and made her teeth meet in Murreyfield's hand. With flashing eyes and tearing fingers she was as fierce as a wild cat at bay. It was with some difficulty that we mastered her, and dragged her — almost carried her — up the stairs. We thrust her into her room and turned the key, while she screamed out abuse and beat upon the door inside.

"It's a forty-foot drop into the garden," said Murreyfield, tying up his bleeding hand. "I'll wait here till you come back. I think we have the lady fairly safe."

"I have a revolver here," said I. "You should be armed." I slipped a couple of cartridges into it and held it out to him. "We can't afford to take chances. How do you know what friends she may have?"

"Thank you," said he. "I have a stick here, and the gardener is within call. Do you hurry off for the guard, and I will answer for the prisoner."

Having taken, as it seemed to me, every possible precaution, I ran to give the alarm. It was two miles to Pedley, and the colonel was out, which occasioned some delay. Then there were formalities and a magistrate's signature to be obtained. A policeman was to serve the warrant, but a military escort was to be sent in to bring back the prisoner. I was so filled with anxiety and impatience that I could not wait, but I hurried back alone with the promise that they would follow.

The Pedley-Woodrow Road opens into the high-road to Colchester at a point about half a mile from the village of Radchurch. It was evening now and the light was such that one could not see more than twenty or thirty yards ahead. I had proceeded only a very short way from the point of junction when I heard, coming towards me, the roar of a motor-cycle being ridden at a furious pace. It was without lights, and close upon me. I sprang aside in order to avoid being ridden down, and in that instant, as the machine flashed by, I saw clearly the face of the rider. It was she — the woman whom I had loved. She was hatless, her hair streaming in the wind, her face glimmering white in the twilight, flying through the night like one of the Valkyries of her native land. She was past me like a flash and tore on down the Colchester Road. In that instant I saw all that it would mean if she could reach the town. If she once was allowed to see her agent we might arrest him or her, but it would be too late. The news would have been passed on. The victory of the Allies and the lives of thousands of our soldiers were at stake. Next instant I had pulled out the loaded revolver and fired two shots after the vanishing figure, already only a dark blur in the dusk. I heard a scream, the crashing of the breaking cycle, and all was still.

I need not tell you more, gentlemen. You know the rest. When I ran forward I found her lying in the ditch. Both of my bullets had struck her. One of them had penetrated her brain. I was still standing beside her body when Murreyfield arrived, running breathlessly down the road. She had, it seemed, with great courage and activity scrambled down the ivy of the wall; only when he heard the whirr of the cycle did he realize what had occurred. He was explaining it to my dazed brain when the police and soldiers arrived to arrest her. By the irony of fate it was me whom they arrested instead.

It was urged at the trial in the police-court that jealousy was the cause of the crime. I did not deny it, nor did I put forward any witnesses to deny it. It was my desire that they should believe it. The hour of the French advance had not yet come, and I could not defend myself without producing the letter which would reveal it. But now it is over — gloriously over — and so my lips are unsealed at last. I confess my fault — my very grievous fault. But it is not that for which you are trying me. It is for murder. I should have thought myself the murderer of my own countrymen if I had let the woman pass. These are the facts, gentlemen. I leave my future in your hands. If you should absolve me I may say that I have hopes of serving my country in a fashion which will atone for this one great indiscretion, and will also, as I hope, end for ever those terrible recollections which weigh me down. If you condemn me, I am ready to face whatever you may think fit to inflict.

X. THREE OF THEM

I — A CHAT ABOUT CHILDREN, SNAKES, AND ZEBUS

These little sketches are called "Three of Them," but there are really five, on and off the stage. There is Daddy, a lumpish person with some gift for playing Indian games when he is in the mood. He is then known as "The Great Chief of the Leatherskin Tribe." Then there is my Lady Sunshine. These are the grown-ups, and don't really count. There remain the three, who need some differentiating upon paper, though their little spirits are as different in reality as spirits could be — all beautiful and all quite different. The eldest is a boy of eight whom we shall call "Laddie." If ever there was a little cavalier sent down ready-made it is he. His soul is the most gallant, unselfish, innocent thing that ever God sent out to get an extra polish upon earth. It dwells in a tall, slight, well-formed body, graceful and agile, with a head and face as clean-cut as if an old Greek cameo had come to life, and a pair of innocent and yet wise grey eyes that read and win the heart. He is shy and does not shine before strangers. I have said that he is unselfish and brave. When there is the usual wrangle about going to bed, up he gets in his sedate way. "I will go first," says he, and off he goes, the eldest, that the others may have the few extra minutes while he is in his bath. As to his courage, he is absolutely lion-hearted where he can help or defend any one else. On one occasion Daddy lost his temper with Dimples (Boy Number 2), and, not without very good provocation, gave him a tap on the side of the head.

Next instant he felt a butt down somewhere in the region of his waist-belt, and there was an angry little red face looking up at him, which turned suddenly to a brown mop of hair as the butt was repeated. No one, not even Daddy, should hit his little brother. Such was Laddie, the gentle and the fearless.

Then there is Dimples. Dimples is nearly seven, and you never saw a rounder, softer, dimplier face, with two great roguish, mischievous eyes of wood-pigeon grey, which are sparkling with fun for the most part, though they can look sad and solemn enough at times. Dimples has the making of a big man in him. He has depth and reserves in his tiny soul. But on the surface he is a boy of boys, always in innocent mischief. "I will now do mischuff," he occasionally announces, and is usually as good as his word. He has a love and understanding of all living creatures, the uglier and more slimy the better, treating them all in a tender, fairylike fashion which seems to come from some inner knowledge. He has been found holding a buttercup under the mouth of a slug "to see if he likes butter." He finds creatures in an astonishing way. Put him in the fairest garden, and presently he will approach you with a newt, a toad, or a huge snail in his custody. Nothing would ever induce him to hurt them, but he gives them what he imagines to be a little treat and then restores them to their homes. He has been known to speak bitterly to the Lady when she has given orders that caterpillars be killed if found upon the cabbages, and even the explanation that the caterpillars were doing the work of what he calls "the Jarmans" did not reconcile him to their fate.

He has an advantage over Laddie, in that he suffers from no trace of shyness and is perfectly friendly in an instant with any one of every class of life, plunging straight into conversation with some such remark as "Can your Daddy give a war-whoop?" or "Were you ever chased by a bear?" He is a sunny creature but combative sometimes, when he draws down his brows, sets his eyes, his chubby cheeks flush, and his lips go back from his almond-white teeth. "I am Swankie the Berserker," says he, quoting out of his favourite "Erling the Bold," which Daddy reads aloud at bed-time. When he is in this fighting mood he can even drive back Laddie, chiefly because the elder is far too chivalrous to hurt him. If you want to see what Laddie can really do, put the small gloves on him and let him go for Daddy. Some of those hurricane rallies of his would stop Daddy grinning if they could get home, and he has to fall back off his stool in order to get away from them.

If that latent power of Dimples should ever come out, how will it be manifest? Surely in his imagination. Tell him a story and the boy is lost. He sits with his little round, rosy face immovable and fixed, while his eyes never budge from those of the speaker. He sucks in everything that is weird or adventurous or wild. Laddie is a rather restless soul, eager to be up and doing; but Dimples is absorbed in the present if there be something worth hearing to be heard. In height he is half a head shorter than his brother, but rather more sturdy in build. The power of his voice is one of his noticeable characteristics. If Dimples is coming you know it well in advance. With that physical gift upon the top of his audacity, and his loquacity, he fairly takes command of any place in which he may find himself, while Laddie, his soul too noble for jealousy, becomes one of the laughing and admiring audience.

Then there is Baby, a dainty elfin Dresden-china little creature of five, as fair as an angel and as deep as a well. The boys are but shallow, sparkling pools compared with this little girl with her self-repression and dainty aloofness. You know the boys, you never feel that you quite know the girl. Something very strong and forceful seems to be at the back of that wee body. Her will is tremendous. Nothing can break or even bend it. Only kind guidance and friendly reasoning can mould it. The boys are helpless if she has really made up her mind. But this is only when she asserts herself, and those are rare occasions. As a rule she sits quiet, aloof, affable, keenly alive to all that passes and yet taking no part in it save for some subtle smile or glance. And then suddenly the wonderful grey-blue eyes under the long black lashes will gleam like coy diamonds, and such a hearty little chuckle will come from her that every one else is bound to laugh out of sympathy. She and Dimples are great allies and yet have continual lovers' quarrels. One night she would not even include his name in her prayers. "God bless — " every one else, but not a word of Dimples. "Come, come, darling!" urged the Lady. "Well, then, God bless horrid Dimples!" said she at last, after she had named the cat, the goat, her dolls, and her Wriggly.

That is a strange trait, the love for the Wriggly. It would repay thought from some scientific brain. It is an old, faded, disused downy from her cot. Yet go where she will, she must take Wriggly with her. All her toys put together would not console her for the absence of Wriggly. If the family go to the seaside, Wriggly must come too. She will not sleep without the absurd bundle in her arms. If she goes to a party she insists upon dragging its disreputable folds along with her, one end always projecting "to give it fresh air." Every phase of childhood represents to the philosopher something in the history of the race. From the new-born baby which can hang easily by one hand from a broomstick with its legs drawn up under it, the whole evolution of mankind is re-enacted. You can trace clearly the cave-dweller, the hunter, the scout. What, then, does Wriggly represent? Fetish worship — nothing else. The savage chooses some most unlikely thing and adores it. This dear little savage adores her Wriggly.

So now we have our three little figures drawn as clearly as a clumsy pen can follow such subtle elusive creatures of mood and fancy. We will suppose now that it is a summer evening, that Daddy is seated smoking in his chair, that the Lady is listening somewhere near, and that the three are in a tumbled heap upon the bear-skin before the empty fireplace trying to puzzle out the little problems of their tiny lives. When three children play with a new thought it is like three kittens with a ball, one giving it a pat and another a pat, as they chase it from point to point. Daddy would interfere as little as possible, save when he was called upon to explain or to deny. It was usually wiser for him to pretend to be doing something else. Then their talk was the more natural. On this occasion, however, he was directly appealed to.

"Daddy!" asked Dimples.

"Yes, boy."

"Do you fink that the roses know us?"

Dimples, in spite of his impish naughtiness, had a way of looking such a perfectly innocent and delightfully kissable little person that one felt he really might be a good deal nearer to the sweet secrets of Nature than his elders. However, Daddy was in a material mood.

"No, boy; how could the roses know us?"

"The big yellow rose at the corner of the gate knows *me*."

"How do you know that?"

"'Cause it nodded to me yesterday."

Laddie roared with laughter.

"That was just the wind, Dimples."

"No, it was not," said Dimples, with conviction. "There was none wind. Baby was there. Weren't you, Baby?"

"The wose knew us," said Baby, gravely.

"Beasts know us," said Laddie. "But them beasts run round and make noises. Roses don't make noises."

"Yes, they do. They rustle."

"Woses wustle," said Baby.

"That's not a living noise. That's an all-the-same noise. Different to Roy, who barks and makes different noises all the time. Fancy the roses all barkin' at you. Daddy, will you tell us about animals?"

That is one of the child stages which takes us back to the old tribe life — their inexhaustible interest in animals, some distant echo of those long nights when wild men sat round the fires and peered out into the darkness, and whispered about all the strange and deadly creatures who fought with them for the lordship of the earth. Children love caves, and they love fires and meals out of doors, and they love animal talk — all relics of the far distant past.

"What is the biggest animal in South America, Daddy?"

Daddy, wearily: "Oh, I don't know."

"I s'pose an elephant would be the biggest?"

"No, boy; there are none in South America."

"Well, then, a rhinoceros?"

"No, there are none."

"Well, what is there, Daddy?"

"Well, dear, there are jaguars. I suppose a jaguar is the biggest."

"Then it must be thirty-six feet long."

"Oh, no, boy; about eight or nine feet with his tail."

"But there are boa-constrictors in South America thirty-six feet long."

"That's different."

"Do you fink," asked Dimples, with his big, solemn, grey eyes wide open, "there was ever a boa-'strictor forty-five feet long?"

"No, dear; I never heard of one."

"Perhaps there was one, but you never heard of it. Do you fink you would have heard of a boa-'strictor forty-five feet long if there was one in South America?"

"Well, there may have been one."

"Daddy," said Laddie, carrying on the cross-examination with the intense earnestness of a child, "could a boa-constrictor swallow any small animal?"

"Yes, of course he could."

"Could he swallow a jaguar?"

"Well, I don't know about that. A jaguar is a very large animal."

"Well, then," asked Dimples, "could a jaguar swallow a boa-'strictor?"

"Silly ass," said Laddie. "If a jaguar was only nine feet long and the boa-constrictor was thirty-five feet long, then there would be a lot sticking out of the jaguar's mouth. How could he swallow that?"

"He'd bite it off," said Dimples. "And then another slice for supper and another for breakfast — but, I say, Daddy, a 'stricter couldn't swallow a porkpine, could he? He would have a sore throat all the way down."

Shrieks of laughter and a welcome rest for Daddy, who turned to his paper.

"Daddy!"

He put down his paper with an air of conscious virtue and lit his pipe.

"Well, dear?"

"What's the biggest snake you ever saw?"

"Oh, bother the snakes! I am tired of them."

But the children were never tired of them. Heredity again, for the snake was the worst enemy of arboreal man.

"Daddy made soup out of a snake," said Laddie. "Tell us about that snake, Daddy."

Children like a story best the fourth or fifth time, so it is never any use to tell them that they know all about it. The story which they can check and correct is their favourite.

"Well, dear, we got a viper and we killed it. Then we wanted the skeleton to keep and we didn't know how to get it. At first we thought we would bury it, but that seemed too slow. Then I had the idea to boil all the viper's flesh off its bones, and I got an old meat-tin and we put the viper and some water into it and put it above the fire."

"You hung it on a hook, Daddy."

"Yes, we hung it on the hook that they put the porridge pot on in Scotland. Then just as it was turning brown in came the farmer's wife, and ran up to see what we were cooking. When she saw the viper she thought we were going to eat it. 'Oh, you dirty divils!' she cried, and caught up the tin in her apron and threw it out of the window."

Fresh shrieks of laughter from the children, and Dimples repeated "You dirty divil!" until Daddy had to clump him playfully on the head.

"Tell us some more about snakes," cried Laddie. "Did you ever see a really dreadful snake?"

"One that would turn you black and dead you in five minutes?" said Dimples. It was always the most awful thing that appealed to Dimples.

"Yes, I have seen some beastly creatures. Once in the Sudan I was dozing on the sand when I opened my eyes and there was a horrid creature like a big slug with horns, short and thick, about a foot long, moving away in front of me."

"What was it, Daddy?" Six eager eyes were turned up to him.

"It was a death-adder. I expect that would dead you in five minutes, Dimples, if it got a bite at you."

"Did you kill it?"

"No; it was gone before I could get to it."

"Which is the horridest, Daddy — a snake or a shark?"

"I'm not very fond of either!"

"Did you ever see a man eaten by sharks?"

"No, dear, but I was not so far off being eaten

myself."

"Oo!" from all three of them.

"I did a silly thing, for I swam round the ship in water where there are many sharks. As I was drying myself on the deck I saw the high fin of a shark above the water a little way off. It had heard the splashing and come up to look for me."

"Weren't you frightened, Daddy?"

"Yes. It made me feel rather cold." There was silence while Daddy saw once more the golden sand of the African beach and the snow-white roaring surf, with the long, smooth swell of the bar.

Children don't like silences.

"Daddy," said Laddie. "Do zebus bite?"

"Zebus! Why, they are cows. No, of course not."

"But a zebu could butt with its horns."

"Oh, yes, it could butt."

"Do you think a zebu could fight a crocodile?"

"Well, I should back the crocodile."

"Why?"

"Well, dear, the crocodile has great teeth and would eat the zebu."

"But suppose the zebu came up when the crocodile was not looking and butted it."

"Well, that would be one up for the zebu. But one butt wouldn't hurt a crocodile."

"No, one wouldn't, would it? But the zebu would keep on. Crocodiles live on sand-banks, don't they? Well, then, the zebu would come and live near the sandbank too — just so far as the crocodile would never see him. Then every time the crocodile wasn't looking the zebu would butt him. Don't you think he would beat the crocodile?"

"Well, perhaps he would."

"How long do you think it would take the zebu to beat the crocodile?"

"Well, it would depend upon how often he got in his butt."

"Well, suppose he butted him once every three hours, don't you think — ?"

"Oh, bother the zebu!"

"That's what the crocodile would say," cried Laddie, clapping his hands.

"Well, I agree with the crocodile," said Daddy.

"And it's time all good children were in bed," said the Lady as the glimmer of the nurse's apron was seen in the gloom.

II — ABOUT CRICKET

Supper was going on down below and all good children should have been long ago in the land of dreams. Yet a curious noise came from above.

"What on earth — ?" asked Daddy.

"Laddie practising cricket," said the Lady, with

the curious clairvoyance of motherhood. "He gets out of bed to bowl. I do wish you would go up and speak seriously to him about it, for it takes quite an hour off his rest."

Daddy departed upon his mission intending to be gruff, and my word, he can be quite gruff when he likes! When he reached the top of the stairs, however, and heard the noise still continue, he walked softly down the landing and peeped in through the half-opened door.

The room was dark save for a night-light. In the dim glimmer he saw a little white-clad figure, slight and supple, taking short steps and swinging its arm in the middle of the room.

"Halloa!" said Daddy.

The white-clad figure turned and ran forward to him.

"Oh, Daddy, how jolly of you to come up!"

Daddy felt that gruffness was not quite so easy as it had seemed.

"Look here! You get into bed!" he said, with the best imitation he could manage.

"Yes, Daddy. But before I go, how is this?" He sprang forward and the arm swung round again in a swift and graceful gesture.

Daddy was a moth-eaten cricketer of sorts, and he took it in with a critical eye.

"Good, Laddie. I like a high action. That's the real Spofforth swing."

"Oh, Daddy, come and talk about cricket!" He was pulled on the side of the bed, and the white figure dived between the sheets.

"Yes; tell us about cwicket!" came a cooing voice from the corner. Dimples was sitting up in his cot.

"You naughty boy! I thought one of you was asleep, anyhow. I mustn't stay. I keep you awake."

"Who was Popoff?" cried Laddie, clutching at his father's sleeve. "Was he a very good bowler?"

"Spofforth was the best bowler that ever walked on to a cricket-field. He was the great Australian Bowler and he taught us a great deal."

"Did he ever kill a dog?" from Dimples.

"No, boy. Why?"

"Because Laddie said there was a bowler so fast that his ball went frue a coat and killed a dog."

"Oh, that's an old yarn. I heard that when I was a little boy about some bowler whose name, I think, was Jackson."

"Was it a big dog?"

"No, no, son; it wasn't a dog at all."

"It was a cat," said Dimples.

"No; I tell you it never happened."

"But tell us about Spofforth," cried Laddie. Dimples, with his imaginative mind, usually wandered, while the elder came eagerly back to the point. "Was he very fast?"

"He could be very fast. I have heard cricketers who had played against him say that his yorker — that is a ball which is just short of a full pitch — was the fastest ball in England. I have myself seen his long arm swing round and the wicket go down before ever the batsman had time to ground his bat."

"Oo!" from both beds.

"He was a tall, thin man, and they called him the Fiend. That means the Devil, you know."

"And *was* he the Devil?"

"No, Dimples, no. They called him that because he did such wonderful things with the ball."

"Can the Devil do wonderful things with a ball?"

Daddy felt that he was propagating devil-worship and hastened to get to safer ground.

"Spofforth taught us how to bowl and Blackham taught us how to keep wicket. When I was young we always had another fielder, called the long-stop, who stood behind the wicket-keeper. I used to be a thick, solid boy, so they put me as long-stop, and the balls used to bounce off me, I remember, as if I had been a mattress."

Delighted laughter.

"But after Blackham came wicket-keepers had to learn that they were there to stop the ball. Even in good second-class cricket there were no more long-stops. We soon found plenty of good wicket-keeps

— like Alfred Lyttelton and MacGregor — but it was Blackham who showed us how. To see Spofforth, all india-rubber and ginger, at one end bowling, and Blackham, with his black beard over the bails waiting for the ball at the other end, was worth living for, I can tell you."

Silence while the boys pondered over this. But Laddie feared Daddy would go, so he quickly got in a question. If Daddy's memory could only be kept going there was no saying how long they might keep him.

"Was there no good bowler until Spofforth came?"

"Oh, plenty, my boy. But he brought something new with him. Especially change of pace — you could never tell by his action up to the last moment whether you were going to get a ball like a flash of lightning, or one that came slow but full of devil and spin. But for mere command of the pitch of a ball I should think Alfred Shaw, of Nottingham, was the greatest bowler I can remember. It was said that he could pitch a ball twice in three times upon a half-crown!"

"Oo!" And then from Dimples: —

"Whose half-crown?"

"Well, anybody's half-crown."

"Did he get the half-crown?"

"No, no; why should he?"

"Because he put the ball on it."

"The half-crown was kept there always for people to aim at," explained Laddie.

"No, no, there never was a half-crown."

Murmurs of remonstrance from both boys.

"I only meant that he could pitch the ball on anything — a half-crown or anything else."

"Daddy," with the energy of one who has a happy idea, "could he have pitched it on the batsman's toe?"

"Yes, boy, I think so."

"Well, then, suppose he *always* pitched it on the batsman's toe!"

Daddy laughed.

"Perhaps that is why dear old W. G. always stood with his left toe cocked up in the air."

"On one leg?"

"No, no, Dimples. With his heel down and his toe up."

"Did you know W. G., Daddy?"

"Oh, yes, I knew him quite well."

"Was he nice?"

"Yes, he was splendid. He was always like a great jolly schoolboy who was hiding behind a huge black beard."

"Whose beard?"

"I meant that he had a great bushy beard. He

looked like the pirate chief in your picture-books, but he had as kind a heart as a child. I have been told that it was the terrible things in this war that really killed him. Grand old W. G.!"

"Was he the best bat in the world, Daddy?"

"Of course he was," said Daddy, beginning to enthuse to the delight of the clever little plotter in the bed. "There never was such a bat — never in the world — and I don't believe there ever could be again. He didn't play on smooth wickets, as they do now. He played where the wickets were all patchy, and you had to watch the ball right on to the bat. You couldn't look at it before it hit the ground and think, 'That's all right. I know where that one will be!' My word, that was cricket. What you got you earned."

"Did you ever see W. G. make a hundred, Daddy?"

"See him! I've fielded out for him and melted on a hot August day while he made a hundred and fifty. There's a pound or two of your Daddy somewhere on that field yet. But I loved to see it, and I was always sorry when he got out for nothing, even if I were playing against him."

"Did he ever get out for nothing?"

"Yes, dear; the first time I ever played in his company he was given out leg-before-wicket before he made a run. And all the way to the pavilion — that's where people go when they are out — he was walking forward, but his big black beard was backward over his shoulder as he told the umpire what he thought."

"And what *did* he think?"

"More than I can tell you, Dimples. But I dare say he was right to be annoyed, for it was a left-handed bowler, bowling round the wicket, and it is very hard to get leg-before to that. However, that's all Greek to you."

"What's Gweek?"

"Well, I mean you can't understand that. Now I am going."

"No, no, Daddy; wait a moment! Tell us about Bonner and the big catch."

"Oh, you know about that!"

Two little coaxing voices came out of the darkness.

"Oh, please! Please!"

"I don't know what your mother will say! What was it you asked?"

"Bonner!"

"Ah, Bonner!" Daddy looked out in the gloom and saw green fields and golden sunlight, and great sportsmen long gone to their rest. "Bonner was a wonderful man. He was a giant in size."

"As big as you, Daddy?"

Daddy seized his elder boy and shook him playfully. "I heard what you said to Miss Cregan the other day. When she asked you what an acre was you said 'About the size of Daddy.'"

Both boys gurgled.

"But Bonner was five inches taller than I. He was a giant, I tell you."

"Did nobody kill him?"

"No, no, Dimples. Not a story-book giant. But a great, strong man. He had a splendid figure and blue eyes and a golden beard, and altogether he was the finest man I have ever seen — except perhaps one."

"Who was the one, Daddy?"

"Well, it was the Emperor Frederick of Germany."

"A Jarman!" cried Dimples, in horror.

"Yes, a German. Mind you, boys, a man may be a very noble man and be a German — though what has become of the noble ones these last three years is more than I can guess. But Frederick was noble and good, as you could see on his face. How he ever came to be the father of such a blasphemous braggart" — Daddy sank into reverie.

"Bonner, Daddy!" said Laddie, and Daddy came back from politics with a start.

"Oh, yes, Bonner. Bonner in white flannels on the green sward with an English June sun upon him. That was a picture of a man! But you asked me about the catch. It was in a test match at the Oval — England against Australia. Bonner said before he went in that he would hit Alfred Shaw into the next county, and he set out to do it. Shaw, as I have told you, could keep a very good length, so for some time Bonner could not get the ball he wanted, but at last he saw his chance, and he jumped out and hit that ball the most awful ker-wallop that ever was seen in a cricket-field."

"Oo!" from both boys: and then, "Did it go into the next county, Daddy?" from Dimples.

"Well, I'm telling you!" said Daddy, who was always testy when one of his stories was interrupted. "Bonner thought he had made the ball a half-volley — that is the best ball to hit — but Shaw had deceived him and the ball was really on the short side. So when Bonner hit it, up and up it went, until it looked as if it were going out of sight into the sky."

"Oo!"

"At first everybody thought it was going far outside the ground. But soon they saw that all the giant's strength had been wasted in hitting the ball so high, and that there was a chance that it would fall within the ropes. The batsmen had run three runs and it was still in the air. Then it was seen that an English fielder was standing on the very edge of the field with his back on the ropes, a white figure against the black line of the people. He stood watching the mighty curve of the ball, and twice he raised his hands together above his head as he did so. Then a third time he raised his hands above his head, and the ball was in them and Bonner was out."

"Why did he raise his hands twice?"

"I don't know. He did so."

"And who was the fielder, Daddy?"

"The fielder was G. F. Grace, the younger brother of W. G. Only a few months afterwards he was a dead man. But he had one grand moment in his life, with twenty thousand people all just mad with excitement. Poor G. F.! He died too soon."

"Did you ever catch a catch like that, Daddy?"

"No, boy. I was never a particularly good fielder."

"Did you never catch a good catch?"

"Well, I won't say that. You see, the best catches are very often flukes, and I remember one awful fluke of that sort."

"Do tell us, Daddy?"

"Well, dear, I was fielding at slip. That is very near the wicket, you know. Woodcock was bowling, and he had the name of being the fastest bowler of England at that time. It was just the beginning of the match and the ball was quite red. Suddenly I saw something like a red flash and there was the ball stuck in my left hand. I had not time to move it. It simply came and stuck."

"Oo!"

"I saw another catch like that. It was done by Ulyett, a fine Yorkshire player — such a big, up-standing fellow. He was bowling, and the batsman — it was an Australian in a test match — hit as hard as ever he could. Ulyett could not have seen it, but he just stuck out his hand and there was the ball."

"Suppose it had hit his body?"

"Well, it would have hurt him."

"Would he have cried?" from Dimples.

"No, boy. That is what games are for, to teach you to take a knock and never show it. Supposing that — "

A step was heard coming along the passage.

"Good gracious, boys, here's Mumty. Shut your eyes this moment. It's all right, dear. I spoke to them very severely and I think they are nearly asleep."

"What have you been talking about?" asked the Lady.

"Cwicket!" cried Dimples.

"It's natural enough," said Daddy; "of course when two boys — "

"Three," said the Lady, as she tucked up the little beds.

III — SPECULATIONS

The three children were sitting together in a bunch upon the rug in the gloaming. Baby was talking so Daddy behind his newspaper pricked up his ears, for the young lady was silent as a rule, and every glimpse of her little mind was of interest. She was nursing the disreputable little downy quilt which she called Wriggly and much preferred to any of her dolls.

"I wonder if they will let Wriggly into heaven,"

she said.

The boys laughed. They generally laughed at what Baby said.

"If they won't I won't go in, either," she added.

"Nor me, neither, if they don't let in my Teddy-bear," said Dimples.

"I'll tell them it is a nice, clean, blue Wriggly," said Baby. "I love my Wriggly." She cooed over it and hugged it.

"What about that, Daddy?" asked Laddie, in his earnest fashion. "Are there toys in heaven, do you think?"

"Of course there are. Everything that can make children happy."

"As many toys as in Hamley's shop?" asked Dimples.

"More," said Daddy, stoutly.

"Oo!" from all three.

"Daddy, dear," said Laddie. "I've been wondering about the deluge."

"Yes, dear. What was it?"

"Well, the story about the Ark. All those animals were in the Ark, just two of each, for forty days. Wasn't that so?"

"That is the story."

"Well, then, what did the carnivorous animals eat?"

One should be honest with children and not put them off with ridiculous explanations. Their questions about such matters are generally much more sensible than their parents' replies.

"Well, dear," said Daddy, weighing his words, "these stories are very, very old. The Jews put them in the Bible, but they got them from the people in Babylon, and the people in Babylon probably got them from some one else away back in the beginning of things. If a story gets passed down like that, one person adds a little and another adds a little, and so you never get things quite as they happened. The Jews put it in the Bible exactly as they heard it, but it had been going about for thousands of years before then."

"So it was not true?"

"Yes, I think it was true. I think there was a great flood, and I think that some people did escape, and that they saved their beasts, just as we should try to save Nigger and the Monkstown cocks and hens if we were flooded out. Then they were able to start again when the waters went down, and they were naturally very grateful to God for their escape."

"What did the people who didn't escape think about it?"

"Well, we can't tell that."

"They wouldn't be very grateful, would they?"

"Their time was come," said Daddy, who was a bit of a Fatalist. "I expect it was the best thing."

"It was jolly hard luck on Noah being swallowed by a fish after all his trouble," said Dimples.

"Silly ass! It was Jonah that was swallowed. Was it a whale, Daddy?"

"A whale! Why, a whale couldn't swallow a herring!"

"A shark, then?"

"Well, there again you have an old story which has got twisted and turned a good deal. No doubt he was a holy man who had some great escape at sea, and then the sailors and others who admired him invented this wonder."

"Daddy," said Dimples, suddenly, "should we do just the same as Jesus did?"

"Yes, dear; He was the noblest Person that ever lived."

"Well, did Jesus lie down every day from twelve to one?"

"I don't know that He did."

"Well, then, I won't lie down from twelve to one."

"If Jesus had been a growing boy and had been ordered to lie down by His Mumty and the doctor, I am sure He would have done so."

"Did He take malt extract?"

"He did what He was told, my son — I am sure of that. He was a good man, so He must have been a good boy — perfect in all He did."

"Baby saw God yesterday," remarked Laddie, casually.

Daddy dropped his paper.

"Yes, we made up our minds we would all lie on our backs and stare at the sky until we saw God. So we put the big rug on the lawn and then we all lay down side by side, and stared and stared. I saw nothing, and Dimples saw nothing, but Baby says she saw God."

Baby nodded in her wise way.

"I saw Him," she said.

"What was He like, then?"

"Oh, just God."

She would say no more, but hugged her Wriggly.

The Lady had entered and listened with some trepidation to the frank audacity of the children's views. Yet the very essence of faith was in that audacity. It was all so unquestionably real.

"Which is strongest, Daddy, God or the Devil?" It was Laddie who was speculating now.

"Why, God rules everything, of course."

"Then why doesn't He kill the Devil?"

"And scalp him?" added Dimples.

"That would stop all trouble, wouldn't it, Daddy?"

Poor Daddy was rather floored. The Lady came

to his help.

"If everything was good and easy in this world, then there would be nothing to fight against, and so, Laddie, our characters would never improve."

"It would be like a football match with all the players on one side," said Daddy.

"If there was nothing bad, then, nothing would be good, for you would have nothing to compare by," added the Lady.

"Well, then," said Laddie, with the remorseless logic of childhood, "if that is so, then the Devil is very useful; so he can't be so very bad, after all."

"Well, I don't see that," Daddy answered. "Our Army can only show how brave it is by fighting the German Emperor, but that does not prove that the German Emperor is a very nice person, does it now?

"Besides," Daddy continued, improving the occasion, "you must not think of the Devil as a person. You must think of all the mean things one could do, and all the dirty things, and all the cruel things, and that is really the Devil you are fighting against. You couldn't call them useful, could you?"

The children thought over this for a little.

"Daddy," said Laddie, "have *you* ever seen God?"

"No, my boy. But I see His works. I expect that is as near as we can get in this world. Look at all the stars at night, and think of the Power that made them and keeps each in its proper place."

"He couldn't keep the shooting stars in their proper place," said Dimples.

"I expect He meant them to shoot," said Laddie.

"Suppose they all shot, what jolly nights we should have!" cried Dimples.

"Yes," said Laddie; "but after one night they would all have gone, and a nice thing then!"

"Well, there's always the moon," remarked Dimples. "But, Daddy, is it true that God listens to all we say?"

"I don't know about that," Daddy answered, cautiously. You never know into what trap those quick little wits may lead you. The Lady was more rash, or more orthodox.

"Yes, dear, He does hear all you say."

"Is He listenin' now?"

"Yes, dear."

"Well, I call it vewy rude of Him!"

Daddy smiled, and the Lady gasped.

"It isn't rude," said Laddie. "It is His duty, and He *has* to notice what you are doing and saying. Daddy, did you ever see a fairy?"

"No, boy."

"I saw one once."

Laddie is the very soul of truth, quite painfully truthful in details, so that his quiet remark caused attention.

"Tell us about it, dear."

He described it with as little emotion as if it were a Persian cat. Perhaps his perfect faith had indeed opened something to his vision.

"It was in the day nursery. There was a stool by the window. The fairy jumped on the stool and then down, and went across the room."

"What was it dressed like?"

"All in grey, with a long cloak. It was about as big as Baby's doll. I could not see its arms, for they were under the cloak."

"Did he look at you?"

"No, he was sideways, and I never really saw his face. He had a little cap. That's the only fairy I ever saw. Of course, there was Father Christmas, if you call him a fairy."

"Daddy, was Father Christmas killed in the war?"

"No, boy."

"Because he has never come since the war began. I expect he is fightin' the Jarmans." It was Dimples who was talking.

"Last time he came," said Laddie, "Daddy said one of his reindeers had hurt its leg in the ruts of the Monkstown Lane. Perhaps that's why he never comes."

"He'll come all right after the war," said Daddy, "and he'll be redder and whiter and jollier than ever." Then Daddy clouded suddenly, for he thought of all those who would be missing when Father Christmas came again. Ten loved ones were dead from that one household. The Lady put out her hand, for she always knew what Daddy was thinking.

"They will be there in spirit, dear."

"Yes, and the jolliest of the lot," said Daddy, stoutly. "We'll have our Father Christmas back and all will be well in England."

"But what do they do in India?" asked Laddie.

"Why, what's wrong with them?"

"How do the sledge and the reindeer get across the sea? All the parcels must get wet."

"Yes, dear, there *have* been several complaints," said Daddy, gravely. "Halloa, here's nurse! Time's up! Off to bed!"

They got up resignedly, for they were really very good children. "Say your prayers here before you go," said the Lady. The three little figures all knelt on the rug, Baby still cuddling her Wriggly.

"You pray, Laddie, and the rest can join in."

"God bless every one I love," said the high, clear child-voice. "And make me a good boy, and thank You so much for all the blessings of to-day. And please take care of Alleyne, who is fighting the Germans, and Uncle Cosmo, who is fighting the Germans, and Uncle Woodie, who is fighting the Germans, and all the others who are fighting the

Germans, and the men on the ships on the sea, and Grandma and Grandpa, and Uncle Pat, and don't ever let Daddy and Mumty die. That's all."

"And please send plenty sugar for the poor people," said Baby, in her unexpected way.

"And a little petrol for Daddy," said Dimples.

"Amen!" said Daddy. And the little figures rose for the good-night kiss.

IV — THE LEATHERSKIN TRIBE

"Daddy!" said the elder boy. "Have you seen wild Indians?"

"Yes, boy."

"Have you ever scalped one?"

"Good gracious, no."

"Has one ever scalped you?" asked Dimples.

"Silly!" said Laddie. "If Daddy had been scalped he wouldn't have all that hair on his head — unless perhaps it grew again!"

"He has none hair on the very top," said Dimples, hovering over the low chair in which Daddy was sitting.

"They didn't scalp you, did they, Daddy?" asked Laddie, with some anxiety.

"I expect Nature will scalp me some of these days."

Both boys were keenly interested. Nature presented itself as some rival chief.

"When?" asked Dimples, eagerly, with the evident intention of being present.

Daddy passed his fingers ruefully through his thinning locks. "Pretty soon, I expect," said he.

"Oo!" said the three children. Laddie was resentful and defiant, but the two younger ones were obviously delighted.

"But I say, Daddy, you said we should have an Indian game after tea. You said it when you wanted us to be so quiet after breakfast. You promised, you know."

It doesn't do to break a promise to children. Daddy rose somewhat wearily from his comfortable chair and put his pipe on the mantelpiece. First he held a conference in secret with Uncle Pat, the most ingenious of playmates. Then he returned to the children. "Collect the tribe," said he. "There is a Council in a quarter of an hour in the big room. Put on your Indian dresses and arm yourselves. The great Chief will be there!"

Sure enough when he entered the big room a quarter of an hour later the tribe of the Leatherskins had assembled. There were four of them, for little rosy Cousin John from next door always came in for an Indian game. They had all Indian dresses with high feathers and wooden clubs or tomahawks. Daddy was in his usual untidy tweeds, but carried a rifle. He was very serious when he entered the room, for one should be very serious in a real good Indian game. Then he raised his rifle slowly over his head in greeting and the four childish voices rang out in the war-cry. It was a prolonged wolfish howl which Dimples had been known to offer to teach elderly ladies in hotel corridors. "You can't be in our tribe without it, you know. There is none body about. Now just try once if you can do it." At this moment there are half-a-dozen elderly people wandering about England who have been made children once more by Laddie and Dimples.

"Hail to the tribe!" cried Daddy.

"Hail, Chief!" answered the voices.

"Red Buffalo!"

"Here!" cried Laddie.

"Black Bear!"

"Here!" cried Dimples.

"White Butterfly!"

"Go on, you silly squaw!" growled Dimples.

"Here," said Baby.

"Prairie Wolf!"

"Here," said little four-year-old John.

"The muster is complete. Make a circle round the camp-fire and we shall drink the firewater of the Palefaces and smoke the pipe of peace."

That was a fearsome joy. The fire-water was ginger-ale drunk out of the bottle, which was gravely passed from hand to hand. At no other time had they ever drunk like that, and it made an occasion of it which was increased by the owlish gravity of Daddy. Then he lit his pipe and it was passed also from one tiny hand to another, Laddie taking a hearty suck at it, which set him coughing, while Baby only touched the end of the amber with her little pink lips. There was dead silence until it had gone round and returned to its owner.

"Warriors of the Leatherskins, why have we come here?" asked Daddy, fingering his rifle.

"Humpty Dumpty," said little John, and the children all began to laugh, but the portentous gravity of Daddy brought them back to the warrior mood.

"The Prairie Wolf has spoken truly," said Daddy. "A wicked Paleface called Humpty Dumpty has taken the prairies which once belonged to the Leatherskins and is now camped upon them and hunting our buffaloes. What shall be his fate? Let each warrior speak in turn."

"Tell him he has jolly well got to clear out," said Laddie.

"That's not Indian talk," cried Dimples, with all his soul in the game. "Kill him, great Chief — him and his squaw, too." The two younger warriors merely laughed and little John repeated "Humpty Dumpty!"

"Quite right! Remember the villain's name!" said Daddy. "Now, then, the whole tribe follows me on the war-trail and we shall teach this Paleface to shoot our buffaloes."

"Look here, we don't want squaws," cried

Dimples, as Baby toddled at the rear of the procession. "You stay in the wigwam and cook."

A piteous cry greeted the suggestion.

"The White Butterfly will come with us and bind up the wounds," said Daddy.

"The squaws are jolly good as torturers," remarked Laddie.

"Really, Daddy, this strikes me as a most immoral game," said the Lady, who had been a sympathetic spectator from a corner, doubtful of the ginger-ale, horrified at the pipe, and delighted at the complete absorption of the children.

"Rather!" said the great Chief, with a sad relapse into the normal. "I suppose that is why they love it so. Now, then, warriors, we go forth on the war-trail. One whoop all together before we start. Capital! Follow me, now, one behind the other. Not a sound! If one gets separated from the others let him give the cry of a night owl and the others will answer with the squeak of the prairie lizard."

"What sort of a squeak, please?"

"Oh, any old squeak will do. You don't walk. Indians trot on the war-path. If you see any man hiding in a bush kill him at once, but don't stop to scalp him — "

"Really, dear!" from the corner.

"The great Queen would rather that you scalp him. Now, then! All ready! Start!"

Away went the line of figures, Daddy stooping

with his rifle at the trail, Laddie and Dimples armed with axes and toy pistols, as tense and serious as any Redskins could be. The other two rather more irresponsible but very much absorbed all the same. The little line of absurd figures wound in and out of the furniture, and out on to the lawn, and round the laurel bushes, and into the yard, and back to the clump of trees. There Daddy stopped and held up his hand with a face that froze the children.

"Are all here?" he asked.

"Yes, yes."

"Hush, warriors! No sound. There is an enemy scout in the bushes ahead. Stay with me, you two. You, Red Buffalo, and you, Black Bear, crawl forward and settle him. See that he makes no sound. What you do must be quick and sudden. When all is clear give the cry of the wood-pigeon, and we will join you."

The two warriors crawled off in most desperate earnest. Daddy leaned on his gun and winked at the Lady, who still hovered fearfully in the background like a dear hen whose chickens were doing wonderful and unaccountable things. The two younger Indians slapped each other and giggled. Presently there came the "coo" of a wood-pigeon from in front. Daddy and the tribe moved forward to where the advance guard were waiting in the bushes.

"Great Chief, we could find no scout," said Laddie.

"There was none person to kill," added Dimples.

The Chief was not surprised, since the scout had been entirely of his own invention. It would not do to admit it, however.

"Have you found his trail?" he asked.

"No, Chief."

"Let me look." Daddy hunted about with a look of preternatural sagacity about him. "Before the snows fell a man passed here with a red head, grey clothes, and a squint in his left eye. His trail shows that his brother has a grocer's shop and his wife smokes cigarettes on the sly."

"Oh, Daddy, how could you read all that?"

"It's easy enough, my son, when you get the knack of it. But look here, we are Indians on the war-trail, and don't you forget it if you value your scalp! Aha, here is Humpty Dumpty's trail!"

Uncle Pat had laid down a paper trail from this point, as Daddy well knew; so now the children were off like a little pack of eager harriers, following in and out among the bushes. Presently they had a rest.

"Great Chief, why does a wicked Paleface leave paper wherever he goes?"

Daddy made a great effort.

"He tears up the wicked letters he has written. Then he writes others even wickeder and tears them up in turn. You can see for yourself that he leaves them wherever he goes. Now, warriors, come along!"

Uncle Pat had dodged all over the limited garden, and the tribe followed his trail. Finally they stopped at a gap in the hedge which leads into the field. There was a little wooden hut in the field, where Daddy used to go and put up a printed cardboard: "WORKING." He found it a very good dodge when he wanted a quiet smoke and a nap. Usually there was nothing else in the field, but this time the Chief pushed the whole tribe hurriedly behind the hedge, and whispered to them to look carefully out between the branches.

In the middle of the field a tripod of sticks supported a kettle. At each side of it was a hunched-up figure in a coloured blanket. Uncle Pat had done his work skilfully and well.

"You must get them before they can reach their rifles," said the Chief. "What about their horses? Black Bear, move down the hedge and bring back word about their horses. If you see none give three whistles."

The whistles were soon heard, and the warrior returned.

"If the horses had been there, what would you have done?"

"Scalped them!" said Dimples.

"Silly ass!" said Laddie. "Who ever heard of a horse's scalp? You would stampede them."

"Of course," said the Chief. "If ever you see a horse grazing, you crawl up to it, spring on its back and then gallop away with your head looking under its neck and only your foot to be seen. Don't you forget it. But we must scupper these rascals on our hunting-grounds."

"Shall we crawl up to them?"

"Yes, crawl up. Then when I give a whoop rush them. Take them alive. I wish to have a word with them first. Carry them into the hut. Go!"

Away went the eager little figures, the chubby babes and the two lithe, active boys. Daddy stood behind the bush watching them. They kept a line and tip-toed along to the camp of the strangers. Then on the Chief's signal they burst into a cry and rushed wildly with waving weapons into the camp of the Palefaces. A moment later the two pillow-made trappers were being dragged off into the hut by the whooping warriors. They were up-ended in one corner when the Chief entered, and the victorious Indians were dancing about in front of them.

"Anybody wounded?" asked the Chief.

"No, no."

"Have you tied their hands?"

With perfect gravity Red Buffalo made movements behind each of the pillows.

"They are tied, great Chief."

"What shall we do with them?"

"Cut off their heads!" shrieked Dimples, who was always the most bloodthirsty of the tribe, though in private life he had been known to weep bitterly over a squashed caterpillar.

"The proper thing is to tie them to a stake," said Laddie.

"What do you mean by killing our buffaloes?" asked Daddy, severely.

The prisoners preserved a sulky silence.

"Shall I shoot the green one?" asked Dimples, presenting his wooden pistol.

"Wait a bit!" said the Chief. "We had best keep one as a hostage and send the other back to say that unless the Chief of the Palefaces pays a ransom within three days — "

But at that moment, as a great romancer used to say, a strange thing happened. There was the sound of a turning key and the whole tribe of the Leatherskins was locked into the hut. A moment later a dreadful face appeared at the window, a face daubed with mud and overhung with grass, which drooped down from under a soft cap. The weird creature danced in triumph, and then stooped to set a light to some paper and shavings near the window.

"Heavens!" cried the Chief. "It is Yellow Snake, the ferocious Chief of the Bottlenoses!"

Flame and smoke were rising outside. It was excellently done and perfectly safe, but too much for the younger warriors. The key turned, the door opened, and two tearful babes were in the arms of the kneeling Lady. Red Buffalo and Black Bear were of sterner stuff.

"I'm not frightened, Daddy," said Laddie, though he looked a little pale.

"Nor me," cried Dimples, hurrying to get out of the hut.

"We'll lock the prisoners up with no food and have a council of war upon them in the morning," said the Chief. "Perhaps we've done enough to-day."

"I rather think you have," said the Lady, as she soothed the poor little sobbing figures.

"That's the worst of having kids to play," said Dimples. "Fancy having a squaw in a war-party!"

"Never mind, we've had a jolly good Indian game," said Laddie, as the sound of a distant bell called them all to the nursery tea.

Footnotes:

[1] The reader is referred to the Preface in connection with this story. — A. C. D.